THE TURTLE STREET TRADING CO.

THE TURTLE STREET TRADING CO.

By
Jill Ross Klevin

SCHOLASTIC INC.
New York Toronto London Auckland Sydney

Text copyright © 1982 by Jill Ross Klevin.
Cover illustration by Jacqueline Rogers.
All rights reserved. Published by Scholastic Inc., 555 Broadway,
New York, NY 10012, by arrangement with Delacorte Press.
Printed in the U.S.A.
ISBN 0-590-20859-4

4 5 6 7 8 9 10   40   12 11 10

For Georgie,
belatedly but with love,
from D.M.K. Swansdowne

THE TURTLE STREET
TRADING CO.

1

The Turtles
in Trouble

It was the hottest day of the summer. Outside it was ninety-five degrees, but inside Mikey McGrath's garage it was closer to a hundred. Morgan J. Pierpont III wiped his face with his T-shirt and banged three times on a packing crate with Mikey's father's hammer.

"This meeting of the Turtles of Turtle Street will now come to order!" he said in his official presidential voice.

The three other Turtles ignored him and went right on with what they were doing. P.J., who was convinced she was John Wayne, kept on moseying around the garage doing her terrible imitation of the Duke in one of his old movies.

"I wanna tell ya, little buddy, we got bushwacked at the pass!" she said several times.

P.J. was all dressed up in her John Wayne outfit—a

cowboy hat so big on her it was always falling down over her nose, a cowboy shirt with fringes, a cowboy belt with a silver buckle, faded jeans, and the cowboy boots with the pointy toes and high heels that her father had sent her from Arizona for her birthday.

Fergy, the fastest eater in the West, was lying on the floor reading a comic and eating his way through a box of Ring Dings. He was eating them fast because he was afraid that if he didn't, somebody else might decide he wanted one, and he would have to share.

Mikey was in the corner playing with Snooky's latest litter of kittens. He was so engrossed, he didn't even hear Morgan. His curly, carroty-red hair was almost as long as P.J.'s. It hung in his eyes, and he had to keep brushing it back so he could see. In summer his freckles all ran together, turning his face into one gigantic freckle.

Morgan didn't even bother to bang on the packing crate again. What was the use? He shook his head in disgust. It was beginning to look as though he, Morgan J. Pierpont III, president elect of the secret society known as the Turtles, was the only one who was serious around here.

"You guys are really something. None of you even cares about this club."

Mikey looked at him with a sad expression in his big blue eyes. "I do, Morg. Honest!"

4

P.J. tripped over a carton marked *Grandma's Dishes*. She looked at him from under her hat and she said, "I do, too. A lot!"

"You sure don't show it," Morgan muttered. He couldn't help feeling guilty. The club had been his idea, a secret society with a secret code and a secret set of bylaws. He had even invented their secret signal, a fist raised in the air with the thumb tucked under the other four fingers to make it look like a turtle's face—if you looked at it from just the right angle and happened to have a good imagination.

Whenever a fellow Turtle made that signal at you, you were supposed to make it back, touch fists three times, then say the secret password: *Turtletaub*! He had even designed their T-shirts and ordered them himself from a catalog his mom had gotten in the mail. On the front was a bright green turtle outlined in orange on a purple background. On the back was their official club motto: *Turtles Together Forever*!

When the kids at school had seen those T-shirts, they had all wanted to join, but the Turtles was a closed society with a limited membership: four. You had to live on Turtle Street to join, and they were the only four kids in the school who did.

The Turtles of Turtle Street. What a super name for a club! All the streets in their neighborhood were named after cold-blooded animals. There was Rattlesnake Road,

Alligator Avenue, Crocodile Court, Lizard Lane, and Salamander Street. You knew whoever had named them was either crazy about cold-blooded animals or had a kid who was.

Morgan felt like a failure. They were supposed to be doing things, going places, being busy, busy, busy every minute. Instead they were sitting here moping. It was summer. There was no school. They had all this free time to devote to having fun, but were they having any fun? No! Because they were, in his father's words, *financially embarrassed*.

"I am bored out of my skull!" P.J. walked over and sat down next to Mikey. One of the kittens started to climb up her leg. She scooped it up, gave it a hug, and put it back in the box beside its mother. It meowed and burrowed in between its brothers and sisters, disappearing from sight.

Fergy polished off the last of the crumbs in the bottom of the Ring Ding box and came over to join them. "Whatever happened to that trip to Disneyland you promised we were going on?" he asked Morgan.

Morgan shrugged. Why did they always count on him to do everything—come up with all the ideas, make all the plans, and do all the work? There were three other members of this organization. Couldn't one of them take a little responsibility for once?

"No money, no Disneyland," Morgan muttered, and

shot Fergy a resentful look. "You wouldn't be bored out of your skull if only we had some money," he said to P.J. "That's our whole problem, Turtles. It can be summed up in a single word: *money!*"

"In case you don't know it, Mr. President, *sir*," P.J. said from under her hat, "it's practically impossible for kids to get their hands on any real money, unless they just happen to stumble across some buried treasure somewhere or decide to go out and rob a bank."

Mikey yanked up one drooping sweat sock. "I know a neat place to dig for buried treasure!" he declared, all ready to grab a shovel and go.

Fergy stretched out his back and put his big feet on the packing crate. "You've heard of the Doberman Gang? We'd be the Turtle Gang!" he said, blinking at Morgan from behind his glasses.

"Wow, Ferguson. That's a real knee-slapper," Morgan said in a sarcastic tone. No doubt about it. Fergy looked like a frog, a fat one with horn-rimmed glasses. He had thick, dark hair straight as sticks, and always looked as though someone had put a bowl on his head and cut all around it, which someone probably *had*, since members of the Weintraub family were always giving one another haircuts.

Morgan banged on the packing crate. "This isn't getting us anywhere, you guys. Let's get on with this meeting."

It suddenly occurred to him. This one could very easily turn out to be their last. And before he could ask P.J. to read the minutes from the last meeting, Fergy yawned and said in an offhand way, "Aw, forget about the meeting! Why don't we just disband?"

2

Are Turtles About to Become Extinct?

Morgan's stomach took an express elevator down to his toes. He stared at Fergy in disbelief. "Are you serious?"

"Of course I'm serious! You gotta be kidding, Pierpont. What's the big deal? It's not a real club anyway. Just because we sit around this smelly garage once a week talking about all the neat things we'd like to do but can't—that doesn't make it a real club."

"And just because we've got matching T-shirts, that doesn't make it a real club either," P.J. put in.

Morgan didn't know what to say. "We can't disband. It's illegal," he offered, for lack of some better reason. "Remember? It says in our bylaws, we're Turtles for life."

P.J. pushed back her hat. "Morgan, for gosh sakes, this

isn't the U.S. Supreme Court or the presidential cabinet. The whole country won't go down the tubes if us four decide to disband our silly club."

"Couldn't we wait a little while longer?" he pleaded. "Like just till the end of the month? Maybe something will come up by then."

The others looked at one another. Morgan held his breath. Finally P.J. said, "Oh, okay. If it means that much to you. Let's get on with this dumb, stupid meeting and get it over with. I have to go and feed True Grit."

Morgan let out his breath in a rush. He felt like a condemned man who had been saved at the last second by a phone call from the governor. He banged on the packing crate and said in his official voice, "Ms. Secretary, will you please read the minutes of the last meeting."

P.J. shot him an amused look and replied, "Yeah, sure, Mr. President, if only I can find 'em." She fished in her pockets and came up with a pathetic-looking piece of notebook paper. She smoothed it out and started reading in a self-conscious voice.

"Minutes of the eighth meeting of the Turtles of Turtle Street, Friday, July sixth. *Ahem!* President Morgan J. Pierpont the third called the meeting to order. Vice-president Michael M. McGrath took attendance. All members were present and accounted for. Secretary P.J. Alberoy the great—ta *daaa!*—read the minutes from the previous week's meeting, which, since half of them had gotten eaten up by her dog Eustace, wound up being pretty brief. The members discussed who is supposed to bring snacks to the meetings. It turned out the only one who does is President Pierpont, who said he couldn't anymore because his mom was getting annoyed at him for snack snitching. President Pierpont moved that members take turns snitching snacks, but Treasurer Weintraub noted that that might not work, since, when it came their turn to snitch them, some members might not be able to find any snacks in their houses to snitch."

A loud knock on the door made them all jump. Sanford, the pest of Turtle Street, stuck his head in and said, "Hiya, guys! What are you guys doin' in here?"

"What does it look like we're doing?" Morgan said to his little brother. "We're having our meeting, and it's a secret and private meeting. So scram, Sanford!"

"It sure is hot out here," Sanford gasped in a weak, pitiful voice. He let his eyes roll up and his tongue hang out to show them just how hot it was.

P.J. took pity on him. "Come on in, Sandy. You can be an honorary Turtle, just for today."

Before Morgan could protest, Sanford scrambled over and sat down next to P.J. He gazed up at her with worshipful eyes. Sanford was eight and still going through his cowboy stage. He wanted to grow up to be John Wayne, too, just like P.J., but so far he hadn't gotten the hang of it as well as she had. P.J. was his number two hero after John Wayne.

Morgan was afraid Sanford might blab what went on at their meeting to the outside world, so he said, "Sanford, I'm going to have to ask you to take an oath and swear never to divulge anything you hear at this meeting to anyone."

"Sure, Morg, but what's *divulge*?"

"To tell or reveal. Do you swear or don't you, Sanford?"

Sanford raised his right hand, pinkie extended, crossed his heart, and said solemnly, "Pinkie swear and cross my heart, I won't *divulge*!"

"Good! Now where were we before we were so rudely interrupted?" Morgan asked.

"Halfway through the minutes from the last meeting," P.J. replied, and went on reading. "The members discussed new business: how to get money. Michael McGrath suggested we all get jobs."

"That's not new business. It's old business!" Fergy muttered.

"Mikey, I keep telling you," P.J. said wearily. We can't get jobs. We haven't got working papers. We won't be old enough to get working papers until we're sixteen."

"Gee, that's a long ways away, P.J.," Mikey said with a dejected look.

Sanford let out a yelp. "Does that mean we're not gonna go to Disneyland?"

"We? Who said anything about *we*?" Morgan said. "You can't go to Disneyland with us, Sanford. Only full-fledged Turtles get to go to Disneyland, and you're not a full-fledged Turtle."

"Oh, yeah? Well, who wants to be a Turtle anyway? Bein' a Turtle is dumb. Disneyland is dumb! It's the dumbest thing I ever heard of," Sanford said, starting to suck his thumb.

"It would cost a lot for us to go to Disneyland," Mikey remarked. "How much did you say it would cost, Fergy?"

"About nine bucks apiece to get in, plus at least another four or five each for extra attractions, souvenirs, and food."

"How much in the club account?" P.J. asked.

Fergy consulted the composition book in which he kept their accounts. "Aside from what we scrounged up for the T-shirts, a buck fifty."

"Scratch one trip to Disneyland!" P.J. groaned.

Sanford burst into song, one of his favorite Beatles numbers: *"Just give me money, yeh, yeh, yeh!"*

Morgan gave him a warning look to shut him up, but Sanford gave out with a few more *yeh's* just to irritate him. They all sat around feeling sorry for themselves for a while. Morgan had to admit this was pretty depressing. Maybe Fergy and P.J. were right, and they ought to disband. They weren't getting anywhere this way.

All of a sudden Fergy started whooping and hollering and kicking his feet in the air. They all stared at him. Was he flipping out, or had he eaten something

13

that disagreed with him? "I've got it! I've got it!" he shouted. Then he jumped up, grabbed P.J., and started dancing her around the garage. Morgan had never seen him so animated.

"What's he got?" Mikey whispered to Morgan.

"Whatever it is, I hope it's not catching," Morgan replied.

Fergy released P.J. She tottered over and stood there, weaving back and forth dizzily. "Not a disease," Fergy said triumphantly. "A way for us to make money and save our club. A way to keep the Turtles from becoming extinct!"

3

Morgan's Brainstorm

Fergy's smile was a mile wide. "I know what you're all thinking. That I'm going to come up with another idea like the last one, the Buried Indian Treasure scheme. But you're wrong. This time it's solid, like the national economy."

"I hope it's solider than *that*!" Sanford mumbled. He was learning all about federal spending in his third grade math class for gifted students.

Fergy sat down on the floor next to Mikey and blinked at Morgan from behind his specs. "We can't get jobs because we're not old enough to get working papers, right?"

"*Right!*" they all chorused.

"But that doesn't mean we can't get money."

"What's that, a riddle?" P.J. muttered sarcastically.

Fergy shook his head. "No, a fact of life. Okay, it's true you have to be sixteen or over to get working papers, but you don't have to be any particular age to go into your own business. Anybody's allowed to go into a business, even someone who's twelve."

Morgan had been only half listening. Now he paid attention. The idea of going into a business had never occurred to him. "What kind of business could four inexperienced kids go into?" he asked.

"I don't know," Fergy replied. "I haven't gotten that far yet."

Morgan nibbled his thumb. Mmm. Let's see. What kind could they go into? They were kids, yes. And inexperienced, sure. But they weren't just any four inexperienced kids. They were the Turtles, and among them, not counting Mikey, they probably had an I.Q. of over five hundred. Of course being smart was only part of being a good businessperson. There were other prerequisites. You also had to be practical, diligent, hardworking, ambitious, and responsible.

How would the Turtles shape up as business people? Starting with himself, *great*! He had all the qualifications. How about the others though? Take Fergy. He was smart as anything, a fast talker, real good with big words. He had a good personality, a terrific sense of humor, and when he wasn't showing off, he was fun to have around. But he was just the opposite of practical, definitely not diligent or hardworking, and about as ambitious as a stone. As for responsible, forget it! He was just like his dad, undependable. He'd promise to meet you somewhere, then forget to show up and take off for the beach instead to watch the sunset or to throw a Frisbee around.

P.J. was brainy; also diligent, hardworking, and super-responsible. Just look at the way she took care of that horse of hers. But she had one drawback: She was the moodiest person alive. She'd go into one of her moods, take off for her barn to commune with her horse, and you wouldn't see her again for a week.

Mikey was the sweetest, most good-natured kid alive, and a great friend. But in the brains department he was a little lacking. If you were counting on him to make a contribution, no way. He'd probably wind up more of a mascot than a business partner.

Even if they could come up with a likely business, business people had to be sharp, dedicated, and dependable. They had to take their responsibilities seriously. They couldn't make dates, then break them or just not show up. They couldn't suddenly decide to take off for parts unknown and leave people stranded. They couldn't get into bad moods and disappear from the face of the earth for weeks at a time. They couldn't sit around under trees daydreaming about faraway places, letting everyone else do their thinking for them. In short they couldn't be like three out of four Turtles!

While Morgan was thinking all this through, P.J., Fergy, and Mikey were deciding what kind of business they wanted to go into.

P.J. said they ought to saddle up True Grit and take kids on pony rides.

"True Grit's a horse, not a pony," Mikey remarked.

"That's no horse. That's a nag!" Fergy said, and whinnied. "My dad and I are going to open up a hang-gliding school someday. Or maybe a scuba-diving school or a surfing school in Hawaii."

Mikey wanted to open a nature-exploring business and charge people for taking them on trips into the wilderness.

Nobody was in the least bit interested in what Sanford wanted, but he told them anyway. "I'll be a TV star, and you guys will be my managers!"

"There's got to be some business we could go into. Come on, Morgan. Think!" P.J. demanded. She thought he was a computer that could churn out all sorts of nifty ideas anytime she pressed a button.

Morgan thought about the most successful businessperson he knew—his dad. His dad was always talking business. Business, business, business, that's all he ever thought about. He owned not one, but three, stores already, and he was thinking about opening a fourth. They all had the same name: Pierpont's Party Supply Store. And they all made money.

Morgan's dad had started from the bottom and

worked his way up from there. He said that if you wanted to be a success in your own business, you had to keep in mind the basic, fundamental principle behind all American big business—*supply and demand*. That meant you had to dream up an idea for a product or service the public really needed—even if it didn't know it yet—make it available, then convince the public that it couldn't live without it.

What product or service could four inexperienced kids make available to the public that somebody else hadn't already made available?

That was a toughie! Right down there on Ventura Boulevard was every conceivable kind of business under the sun except one: a business run exclusively by and especially for kids.

That was it, the perfect business for them to go into: a business just for kids. At least they knew something about kids. Not like some other businesses, about which they knew nothing. Let's see, what kind of kids' business could it be? That depended on what kids in this area needed and wanted but didn't already have.

Did Morgan know any kids? Normal ones?

Sanford was a kid, a kid who collected all kinds of junk. If it was junk, and it cost money, he nagged their parents into buying it for him. Of course once he got it he didn't want it anymore and started nagging for something else. And what happened to all that junk he lost interest in? It got stashed away in a carton in the back of their closet, that's what.

A light bulb went on inside Morgan's head. What if, instead of getting stashed away, their old junk could be recycled instead?

"You know," he said as casually as he could under the circumstances, "I was reading just the other day. Kids make up fifty percent of the population in this area."

"How fascinating!" P.J. exclaimed. "But just what does that handy-dandy bit of information have to do with us?"

"Oh, nothing much, only, in my opinion, a business just for kids would probably stand a pretty good chance of making it in a place where kids make up half the population."

Morgan explained his idea. Fergy's eyes narrowed behind his spectacles, and he said, "You mean you want us to go into the junk-recycling business?"

"More like the junk-trading business. Don't you get it, you guys? A trading company where kids could come and bring in all their old junk and trade it for other junk brought in by other kids. I'm talking about a big-time operation here. We could all wind up tycoons!"

P.J. lifted her skinny shoulders in a shrug. "Sounds more like a public service to me."

"That too," Morgan exclaimed. "It's very ecological. While we're providing a unique service to our customers, we'll also be helping the environment by conserving natural resources."

"It's not a bad idea, I guess," P.J. said halfheartedly.

"I think it's good!" Mikey put in, but he always said what he thought Morgan wanted him to, so his opinion didn't really count.

Morgan looked at Fergy. "Well?"

Fergy regarded him with those froggy eyes of his, but he didn't say anything. Not for a couple of minutes, a couple of very long minutes. Then after giving it his careful consideration, he uttered one single word: "*Wow!*"

Morgan grinned delightedly. That one word said it all.

4

Working Things Out

"Fergy liked it. That must mean it's good," Mikey said to Morgan.

Morgan started straightening out the stuff in Mikey's father's tool chest. What a mess! Basically he was a very orderly person. Messy things bothered him. He liked things to be neat. "I don't need him to tell me that. I know it already," he said.

"I don't get it," P.J. interjected. "Just how would this thing work?"

"It's not terribly complicated, P.J.," Morgan replied in a condescending tone. "Not like Elementary Algebra or Plane Geometry or something like that. I'll explain," he went on, figuring he would work out the details as he went along. "Let's say a kid comes into our trading company with something he wants to trade."

"Like what, Morgan?" Sanford piped up.

"Um, let's say it's a kite, okay?"

"A new one or an old, beat-up one, Morgan?"

"Stow it, Sanford. Don't be a pest." Boy, Mr. McGrath's tool box sure was messy! Morgan started with the nails. He lined the largest ones up first, then started on the next-to-largest size. "Say this kid brings in this kite. We look it over. We put a value on it. We tell him it's worth that amount and he can trade it for anything we have worth the same amount."

"Anything we have *where*?" P.J. asked.

Morgan frowned. "Good question! In our inventory, that's where."

"Where do we get the inventory from?" Mikey asked.

"Out of the air," P.J. mumbled.

"Out of our garages is more like it," Fergy added. "Mine's so full of junk, it looks like the Pasadena Flea Market on alternate Sundays. My dad would probably pay us to take it away—if he had any money, that is."

"Wait a sec. I have a question," P.J. put in. "What if this kid with the kite didn't want to trade it in for something worth the same amount? What if he wanted to trade it for something worth more?"

"He could pay us the difference in cash," Morgan replied. "We have nothing against money."

"But what if he wanted to trade it for something worth less, Mr. Smarty?"

Morgan hesitated for a minute. They couldn't go

around giving their customers money. They wouldn't be in business long if they did that. "We'll give them credit," he concluded, feeling pretty proud of himself for solving that one.

"Then," Morgan went on, "our customers will pay us a certain percentage for providing this service to them. That amount will be our commission. Don't you get it, Mikey?" he added when he saw that Mikey was still confused.

Morgan decided to try a different approach. "Look, Mikey, pretend we're open for business, okay? A kid comes in, the one with the kite. Remember him? Riiiight! He wants to trade his kite for something else. We look the kite over. We decide what it's worth—a dollar. We say to the kid, 'Okay, your kite's worth a dollar. That means you can trade it in for anything we have in our inventory worth a dollar.'"

"Inventory?" Mikey interjected.

"Yeah, inventory. Remember, we said it would come out of our garages?" Morgan explained very patiently. "To start off with, we'll provide the inventory. Once the business gets going, and our customers bring in stuff to trade, that will be our inventory. Okay, let's say the kid looks through all our inventory and can't find anything he wants worth one dollar. We tell him he can trade his kite for something worth more if he wants to, or something worth less. If he decides to trade it for something worth more, he pays us the difference in cash. If it's worth a dollar fifty, he gives us back fifty cents, right? Right! If he decides to trade for something worth less, we don't give him the difference in cash. We give him a credit and tell him he can come back and use it up another time."

"What's a credit?" Sanford asked.

"A little piece of paper saying that we owe him a certain amount," Morgan explained to him. "You know, like the credit slips Mom gets when she returns something at the department store? Okay, do we all get it so far? Good! Now, moving right along here, we go on to the question of how much commission we ought to charge for our unique and original service. Say we decide it ought to be ten percent. That means that on a kite for one dollar we get ten cents just for providing the service."

Morgan smiled at his fellow Turtles. Spouting all these business ideas made him feel like a big tycoon already.

"Ten percent isn't enough of a commission for us to charge our customers," Fergy said. "We'll never make any money charging ten percent. We have to charge more; say, twenty or twenty-five percent."

Morgan chewed his lip thoughtfully. Twenty-five percent sounded pretty exorbitant. Maybe their customers would think they were trying to cheat them if they charged that much.

"They'll just think we're smart businessmen," Fergy said when Morgan pointed that out to him.

"Businesspersons," P.J. said.

"Ex-cuse *me, Ms.* Alberoy," Fergy said, and doffed an imaginary hat in her direction. P.J. put her nose in the air and turned her back on him to show how little he or his ideas meant to her.

"I still say ten percent is enough," Morgan said, eager to get back to the business at hand.

"And I say it ought to be twenty-five," Fergy argued.

"Who's the financial wizard around here anyway, me or you?"

"You, I guess," Morgan replied, not all that convinced.

Mikey crept over closer to him and asked, "What's *inventory*, Morgan? Tell me again. I forgot."

"All the stuff we'll have on hand to trade for the stuff our customers bring in," Morgan replied.

"I get it," Sanford said. "You've got good ideas, Morg. You're real smart, you know it? Could I ask you guys a favor, huh? Could I be in the business too? Could I be a partner in your business? 'Cause if you let me, I'll let you have all my toys, I promise."

Morgan looked at the others. "You guys don't want this little creep as a business partner, do you?" He didn't, anyway. Sanford as a kid brother was enough. As a business partner? Too much!

Mikey grinned at Sanford. "We could use the extra person to help out in the business, couldn't we?"

"But such a little extra person, Mikey?" P.J. said, just to tease Sanford.

Sanford started to sulk. He always sulked when he didn't get his way. "How come you don't take a vote, like always? You ought to vote about me bein' in the business, not just ask each other. That's fairer!"

"Okay, Sanford, we'll take a vote," Morgan said, and asked for a show of hands. It was four out of four in favor of letting Sanford into the business, but not as a full partner; just as a part-time helper.

"How come?" Sanford shouted at them.

P.J. explained to him. For some unknown reason, she was crazy about the little jerk, so, when she spoke to him, she always spoke very kindly and didn't act snotty like she sometimes did. "Look, Sandy, that's the law. It says that right in our club bylaws—that only a full-fledged Turtle is entitled to take part in club activities. I'm not saying you can never be a full-fledged Turtle, just that you're not ready to be one now. See, you haven't proven yourself worthy yet. For the time being you can be an honorary Turtle, okay? That means you can be in the business with us. You can even share in the profits like the rest of us. But as far as being a full-fledged Turtle, initiated into the club and into Turtledom, I think you have a long way to go before you're ready for that, Sandy."

"I understand," Sanford said soberly, smiling at her through his tears. "You'll see. I'm gonna prove myself like anything. I'm gonna prove myself so much, you'll

27

be beggin' me to be full-flegged. See, it's not bein' in the business and makin' lots of money that matters to me. It's bein' a full-flegged Turtle!"

They all congratulated him on being an honorary Turtle. Sanford liked that. He liked being the center of attention for whatever reason. Finally Morgan made the official announcement to end the meeting so they could all go home and start rounding up some inventory for their new business.

"Now maybe I can get rid of all that disgusting girly-girly stuff my mother is always buying me," P.J. said.

"Dolls, doll houses, cooking thingees, and stuff. Cripes, I ask for a six-gun for Christmas, and what does she give me? A baby doll that cries and wets it pants. Ugh! How unliberated can you get?" She headed out of the garage.

"Maybe she's not unliberated," Mikey called after her. "Maybe she just doesn't like violence."

"Naw, that's not it," Fergy laughed. "Her mom just keeps hoping P.J.'ll get the hint and turn into a girl."

P.J. stopped in her tracks. Slowly she turned and stared him down, eyes smoldering. Then she said, "Maybe you ought to shut your trap, Hippo Boy, before I belt you one!"

Fergy pretended to be scared. He ducked behind Morgan so P.J. couldn't get to him and pleaded for his life. "Please, pretty please, don't hurt me!" Morgan was afraid P.J. would really lose her temper and threaten to resign from the club, the way she had the last time they had had a major confrontation. But luckily, just at that exact moment, a horse whinnied in the distance. It was True Grit. Without another word P.J. took off down Turtle Street to be with her favorite friend of all time, her horse.

5

All for a
Good Cause

"**M**organ? Sandy? What are you two boys doing in the closet?"

Morgan peeked through the door. It was open a crack, just enough for him to get a glimpse of one red and white jogging shoe. He hadn't heard his mother come upstairs. He put his finger to his lips to keep Sanford, the blurter, from blurting out something stupid and said, "Looking for our Halloween costumes, Mom!"

Sanford kept quiet for once. The only sound in the closet was his breathing noisily through his mouth. Morgan wondered if stuffy closets were good places for little kids with allergies.

"Looking for Halloween costumes?" his mom repeated, and burst out laughing. "In the middle of July? All right, but don't make a mess in there. And don't be long. Dinner's almost ready, and your father will be home any minute."

The jogging shoe made a sharp right, and their mother marched out of the room. Morgan picked up his baseball glove, the one his dad had bought him the year he got elected captain of his Little League team. A lot of fond memories went with that glove. Could he bear to part with it? He probably wouldn't get all that much chance to play ball from now on. Business people were too busy to play ball, and it was a super addition to their inventory.

Sanford held up a matchstick car for his inspection. Morgan dumped it, and the baseball glove, in the carton along with the other stuff they had collected—Sanford's Mr. Mystery game, a model airplane with one wing missing, a model of C-3PO, and two of Sanford's "I Can Read" books.

If the little creep could part with his C-3PO, Morgan supposed he could give up his Mickey Mouse hat and his crazy glasses. Anyway, it was all for a good cause.

Sanford was starting to sniffle. Matter of fact, his nose was kind of red. When he saw Morgan looking at it, he said, "Mothballs! Am I 'lergick to mothballs, Morgan?"

"How am I supposed to know? Am I your doctor? Maybe we better get out of here, just in case." He got up and walked out of the closet. He expected Sanford to follow suit, but he didn't. Or rather, he didn't get up and walk out. He crawled out on his hands and knees. He kept right on crawling across the room, out the door, and down the hallway to the top of the stairs. Even then he didn't get up and walk down them. He slithered down them on his belly, honking and clapping like a seal. He slithered straight through the living room and the dining room and into the kitchen, where Morgan's parents were preparing dinner. When they saw him, they both broke up. For some mysterious reason, they thought Sanford was a terrific comedian.

"Look. It's Sanford the Seal!" Morgan's dad laughed.

"And Morgan the Magnificent, his trainer," Morgan's mom added. She didn't like to give more attention to one than to the other. She thought it made them even more jealous of each other than they already were. She took a pan of broiled fish out of the oven. When Sanford the Seal saw the fish, he stopped honking and clapping and made a face instead.

"Yuk! Fish again?"

"You're a seal," Morgan reminded him, "Seals love fish."

"Yeah? Well, tough, 'cause I'm the one seal who doesn't. I'm the seal who loves hambrugers. I love hambrugers more 'n anything. I love 'em so much, I could eat 'em every single night of the week!"

"Ham*burgers*, not *brugers*, dopey. And that wouldn't

be good for you. Beef's loaded with cholesterol, and too much cholesterol in your diet is unhealthy. It builds up fat in your arteries. Fish hasn't got any cholesterol, so it's healthier than beef."

"Too bad! What if I like chles-ter-roll?" Sanford made a face at Morgan behind their parents' backs and went off to set the table.

While they were having dinner, Morgan's mom said, "I hope you boys aren't giving any of your things away."

Morgan shot Sanford a warning look. He didn't like to lie, especially to his parents. Maybe he'd better tell them the truth. They might tell him to leave the things at home, but he would have to take that chance. If they did, the Turtles would just have to manage with less inventory, that's all.

"Not giving, Mom. Trading," he said, and reached for the broccoli. "We're going to use it as inventory for our new business, the *Turtles'* new business."

His dad's ears perked up when he heard the magic word. "Business? What kind of business, son?"

"A trading company for kids, Dad," Morgan replied, and explained his idea. He could tell his dad was impressed. He kept interrupting Morgan, asking all kinds of questions.

"How will you make any money in this trading business?"

"We'll charge each customer a commission for the

service we're providing, a certain percentage of the value we put on the item, or items, he or she brings in to trade," Morgan said.

"How much of a commission will you charge?" his dad wanted to know. When Morgan told him ten percent, he looked dubious, but he didn't say anything. "I like your idea very much," he went on, respect in his tone. "You're a very enterprising young man, isn't he, Sarah? *Very* enterprising!"

That was the ultimate compliment. Morgan felt proud that his dad thought he was enterprising. When his dad asked if he could help, Morgan didn't yell *"No!"* right off. He tried to be a little more diplomatic.

"Thanks, Dad, but we want to do this ourselves," he said with a smile. He thought of the times he had asked his dad for help—that time his Little League team had needed a coach; the time his class had needed someone to drive for a field trip to the planetarium; the time his boy scout troop had been looking for an assistant den master. All those times his dad had turned him down, saying he was too busy at the store and couldn't spare the time.

"I can't leave the store to go running around with a bunch of kids," he had said to Morgan's mom. Usually he tried to talk her into doing it instead, which was pretty laughable and highly unliberated of him. She had a full-time career, too, didn't she? If he couldn't spare the time, how did he expect her to?

She was a journalist, a staff reporter on *The Valley Herald*, the biggest local newspaper, and the one with the highest circulation. Her career was very important to her, just as important as Morgan's dad's business was to him. She worked hard and put in a lot of hours, sometimes at pretty weird times too. If a story broke, and her boss called her up and asked her to go and cover it, she went, even if it was three o'clock in the morning. She said that was part of what being a journalist was all about.

If there was one thing Morgan wasn't planning on doing, it was asking any grown-ups for help. This was something the Turtles had to do on their own, because when they were successful, the success would be their own and not somebody else's—some grown-up's like his dad's for instance.

He wanted to show his dad he really was enterprising. The idea was terrific, but it wasn't enough just to come up with a terrific idea. You had to turn the idea into a reality, then make it a success. When Morgan had done that, his dad would know just how enterprising he was.

6

Getting It
Together

"**D**ad really liked your idea, Morgan," Sanford said when they were heading down Turtle Street later. "He said it was entersurprising."

"Enterprising, not *sur*prising, Sanford; and it is." Morgan reached over and removed Sanford's thumb from his mouth. It made a popping sound like a cork coming out of a bottle. They were passing Mikey's house. Mrs. McGrath was in the front yard talking to her roses. She held one up for them to see.

"How do you like my new Lavinia Elizabeth? Isn't she a beauty?"

"Nice rose, Mrs. McGrath," Morgan called. He couldn't figure out why anyone would talk to a rose. Dogs or cats, sure. Caterpillars, maybe. But roses?

Sanford's thumb was back in his mouth again. He was sucking noisily away. It didn't faze him one bit to walk into Fergy's living room, where there were at least two dozen people sprawled out all over the floor, with that dumb thumb stuck in his dumb mouth. Fergy had two older brothers and two older sisters. His brothers and sisters had tons of friends. All the friends hung out at Fergy's all the time. They never went home, ever. They ate up all the food—what there was of it—and turned the place into a disaster zone. It always looked like the immediate aftermath of an earthquake.

It was funny, but Fergy and his brothers and sisters all looked alike, kind of pudgy with straight dark hair and big brown eyes, but Mr. Weintraub was tall, skinny, and blond with blue eyes, all of which led Morgan to believe that the kids must all look like their mom. Of course he couldn't be sure. He had never seen their mom. She lived up in San Francisco. She and Mr. Weintraub had been divorced for years.

Whenever you were at Fergy's, you felt invisible. Nobody paid the slightest bit of attention to you. You almost felt you could walk right through the walls; the furniture, too—only there wasn't any.

Morgan went over to Fergy's oldest brother, Filmore. "Have you seen Fergy?"

Filmore didn't respond. He just sat there staring into space and strumming his guitar.

"You haven't seen Fergy, have you?" Morgan asked Fiona, Fergy's fourteen-year-old sister. Fiona looked right through him and went on with what she was doing, eating peanut butter out of a jar with her fingers.

"Have you seen Fergy around?" he asked Felicia, Fergy's oldest sister, who was eighteen. She was over in the corner with her boyfriend, doing her homework. She was the only Weintraub other than Fergy who was even slightly tuned into what was going on in the real world. She looked up from the book she was reading, saw Sanford, and her eyes lit up and said "Tilt!" She was wild about him. That was because he was little and cute and pudgy. When he got older and thinned out, she'd probably ignore him the way she ignored Morgan and the other Turtles. In the meantime, whenever she saw him, all she wanted to do was hug him and kiss him. And when Sanford saw her, he practically frothed at the mouth.

"Fergy's out in the garage," Felicia said, and made a grab for Sanford. He took off for the kitchen, jet-propelled. "Isn't he precious? she said, giggling.

Morgan caught up with Sanford in the garage, gave him a pinch on his pudgy-wudgy cheek, and cooed, "Oooh, isn't he *precious*?"

Sanford ducked behind an old dismantled motorcycle that somebody was trying to rebuild against all odds. Morgan looked at all the corroded spare parts scattered over the floor and muttered, "Lots of luck!"

The garage did resemble the Pasadena Flea Market. It held wall-to-wall junk of every description. No wonder Mr. Weintraub always had to park his pickup truck on the front lawn. Morgan looked around for Fergy. He finally found him halfway in a carton, throwing stuff out right and left. All kinds of things were flying around: toys, books, games, models, records, old clothes, some pathetic-looking stuffed animals—even a beat-up old guitar.

They packed up all the stuff and were dragging it outside when Mr. Weintraub came along. He looked exactly like Buffalo Bill with his shoulder-length blond curls and droopy mustache.

"My dad lost his job again," Fergy confided when they were on their way to Mikey's. "That's the third job he's lost in the past four months. I guess he's not cut out to be a used-car salesman."

"Guess not," Morgan said sympathetically. Mr. Weintraub's losing his job was nothing new. He did that on a regular basis, about once a month. He was a great guy and a great musician—a guitar picker—but Fergy was right. As a used-car salesman, he was a bust.

P.J. and Mikey were already at Mikey's garage, and they had each brought a bunch of stuff. With what Fergy had brought and Morgan and Sanford had collected, they probably had enough inventory to last until Christmas!

"We have to think of a name for our business," Morgan said to the others when they were all finished oohing and aahing over what was in the cartons. "Something snazzy and catchy that'll make people sit up and take notice."

"I know! Turtle Traders," P.J. offered.

"That's snazzy, all right," Fergy sniggered. "But it makes us sound like we trade turtles. That's inhumane!"

"Turtles of America? Turtles, Unlimited? Turtles, Inc.? Come on, you guys. *Think!*" P.J. ordered.

"Listen," Fergy said. "Since we're kids, and we're opening up a business for kids, shouldn't the name of the company have the word *kids* in it?"

"Kids of America? Kids, Unlimited? Kids, Inc?" P.J. started up again. "How about Kidco? Or Kid Traders?"

"We don't trade kids *or* turtles, dummy," Fergy said, and guffawed. "Maybe we ought to, huh?"

"Kid Turtles?" Morgan offered. "Uh uh! That's no good. It doesn't say what kind of business we're in, what we do, or who we are."

"Why don't we put the initials of all our last names together to make a new word and call it that?" P.J. suggested. She got out her notebook and started scribbling, then held it up for them to see.

"A.P.M.W.," she had written on top of a page. Then, underneath that, "WAPM." A bunch of other possibilities followed, all variations on the same general idea:

WAMPUM, INCORPORATED
PAWM
PWAM
APWAM
MAWAP
MAWP

"Okay, forget initials," she muttered, and put the note-book away.

"P.J., why don't you stick to the physical stuff and leave the thinking to us?" Fergy remarked. She gave him a murderous look, and he added, "I didn't meant it, Ms. Muscles. Don't hit me, pretty please?"

Sanford wanted to call it Duke's in honor of his hero, John Wayne, but the others vetoed that. Duke's could just as easily be a service station or a bar and grill as a kid's trading company.

"This is too hard," Sanford decided, and went off to play with Snooky's kittens.

"You're allergic to cats, remember?" Morgan cautioned.

"Cats, not kittens," Sanford replied, and started conversing with Snooky about the joys of motherhood.

P.J. yawned. "Let's take this up again some other time, shall we? I'm too tired to think."

"Hey, don't procrastinate!" Morgan declared. "We have to come up with something now. We can't do anything more until we have a name. We can't put up signs advertising the Something-Something-Something Trading Company."

All this time Mikey had been concentrating hard. You could tell he was by the way his face was all scrunched up in a frown of concentration. "I've got it! I've got it!" he cried excitedly. Nobody paid much attention. In the New and Novel Ideas Department, he wasn't giving any of them much competition. When he said "How about Turtle Trading Company?" nobody exactly fainted from ecstasy. But when he said, "No, the Turtle *Street* Trading Company," they started to pay attention.

P.J. turned it into a song, singing it to the tune of "Frère Jacques."

> *"Turtle Street Trading Company,*
> *Turtle Street Trading Company,*
> *You're true blue,*
> *You're true blooooo!"*

"It has a nice ring to it!" Fergy announced after a moment's deliberation. "Not bad for an amateur, Mikey."

Morgan had to hand it to Mikey. Even he couldn't have come up with a better name. *The Turtle Street Trading Company.* It had a good, solid, bona fide business sound to it. It sounded like tons of customers and money in the bank. It would look super on signs, in ads in newspapers and magazines, and printed on business cards and stationary.

"What do you guys think?" he asked P.J. and Fergy. "It sounds like a winner to me."

They both agreed wholeheartedly, so it was unanimous. Sanford came over. He was sniffling up a storm, rubbing at his nose, and his eyes were tearing. "Thuh Durdle Streed Dradink Compandy," he said in a nasal twang. "*Hooraaaaay!*"

7

Getting
Started

They had a name. Now they needed a place. The next morning they trekked down to Mulview Shopping Center to look over Ralph's parking lot. Okay—Morgan admitted it—a parking lot wasn't the most elegant or beautiful place for a business, but it has one important plus no other place they could think of had. It was free.

When they got back to Turtle Street, Morgan sat down under a tree in his backyard and started making a list.

THINGS TO DO:
1) Borrow a table and chairs.
2) Buy poster board and marking pens for making signs.
3) Buy price stickers to put on things in our inventory.

4) Put an ad in *The Pennysaver* announcing our grand opening.
5) Try and scrounge up some stuff to give away as free prizes.
6) Free refreshments????
7) Famous celebrity for opening day.

When he showed the others his list, P.J. said, "You gotta be putting me on! A celebrity? Who did you have in mind, John Travolta? Sorry, but he's busy that day."

"Call him anyway," Fergy suggested. "Maybe he'll change his plans. My dad knows some celebrities. Why don't we ask him to get us someone? What's this with the free prizes and refreshments? I mean, come on, Morg! We're just poor, starving people going into a new business, not millionaires."

"It doesn't matter," Morgan informed him. "Like my dad's always saying, you have to think big. You have to spend money to make money."

Fergy gave him a look. "Always has to show he knows everything," they heard him mutter as he walked away.

"He's just upset because his dad lost his job again," P.J. said to Morgan, making an excuse for Fergy's behavior. Morgan couldn't figure it out. How come behind Fergy's back she was kind, but to his face she was so mean to him?

Morgan told her that they would need some working

capital to start off with. Not a lot, just enough to buy poster board and marking pens to make some signs, stickers to put on the items in their inventory, and enough to pay for an ad in *The Pennysaver* announcing their grand opening.

"If we had money, we wouldn't need to go into business in the first place," P.J. pointed out.

"I'm only talking about twenty-five dollars, P.J.," he replied. "It would have cost twice that much for all of us to go to Disneyland for a day."

"Just how do you propose to get said twenty-five dollars?" she asked sweetly, and smiled at him the way people usually smiled at dopey little kids who didn't know anything.

"Take out a loan. What else?" he said matter-of-factly.

"Who from—if you don't mind my asking?" she inquired archly. "Are you planning on walking into a bank and asking for a loan of twenty-five dollars?"

"No, I'm planning on walking into Fergy's house and asking his sister Felicia for a loan of twenty-five dollars," Morgan replied. "Remember, Felicia's the miser in the Weintraub family. The rest of them may be broke, but she always has money. She squirrels it away in all sorts of places. She's safer and more dependable than any bank."

Felicia, alias The Miser, was in the hammock in her backyard with her boyfriend, swinging and drinking iced tea to keep cool. Morgan knew the right strategy to use on her. Instead of going over there and asking her himself, he sent Sanford to do it.

"Twenty-five dollars?" Felicia screeched, as though it were all the money in the world. You could hear her all the way to Dallas, Texas, her voice was so shrill and loud. "What could you possibly want with so much money, Sanford?"

"It's for the Turtles' new bizness," Sanford replied, and looked up at her with his big cocker spaniel eyes. He snuggled up and let her give him a little hug, but he stopped short of kissing. You could see what a big sacrifice he was making. The poor kid was writhing with discomfort. Morgan figured it was time for him to intercede and clinch the deal with a little of his fancy fast talk.

"Sounds like a good investment," Felicia's boyfriend commented after Morgan had explained everything in detail. "I'd invest in it if I had any money, which I don't. Hey, give them the twenty-five dollars, Fel, but charge them interest on it."

"You don't have to tell me that. Of course I'll charge them interest. Why should I lend out money if there's nothing in it for me?"

"How much interest would you charge?" Morgan asked.

"The banks are charging twenty percent," she replied, dollar signs appearing in her eyes.

"How about five?"

"How about sixteen?"

47

"Make it five, you've got a deal."

"Make it six, and you have!"

"Okay, six. Boy, you're some shrewd businessperson, Felicia, you know it? If you ever want to invest in a business, we might find a place for you at the Turtle Street Trading Company."

When they got back to Mikey's, he wrote in his notebook: July 14—*Borrowed from Felicia Weintraub the sum of twenty-five dollars ($25.00) at six percent (6%) interest.* Under that he worked out how much interest they would have to pay. *$25.00 @ .06% = $1.50 interest.* It seemed like a lot to pay just to use someone's money for a few days, but they didn't have much of a choice.

"We've got to keep our overhead low," he said to the others. "Twenty-five dollars won't go very far. Not with the prices of things these days."

Sanford was trotting around and around in a circle on an imaginary horse. When he trotted by Mikey, Mikey yelled, "Hi, ho, Silver. Awaaay!"

Sanford looked at him scornfully. "I'm not the Lone Ranger, stupid. I'm the Duke. Can't you tell the difference?" He trotted over to Morgan and asked, "Morgan, what's *overheard*?"

"Not *overheard*. *Overhead*, Sanford," Morgan replied. "That's all our expenses. Everything we spend on our business, like supplies, advertising costs, and so forth. If we were renting a place and fixing it up, that would all be part of our overhead too."

"Are we going to pay ourselves salaries?" Mikey wanted to know.

"No, we'll divide the profits equally among us," Morgan said. "Each one of us gets an equal share, even Sanford."

"Thanks a lot, Pilgrim," Sanford drawled, trying to sound like P.J. sounding like John Wayne.

"We ought to elect officers, I guess," Morgan remarked, and started writing in his notebook. *Officers: president, vice-president, secretary, treasurer, sales manager, advertising manager...*

P.J. peeked over his shoulder. "That's six jobs, and there are only five of us, counting Sandy. How do you figure that, Morgan?"

He shrugged. "We can double up."

"Double Bubble! I wanna be prezdent," Sanford said, and reined in his mount.

"I'll be treasurer, same as before," Fergy announced. "I like being treasurer. Money fascinates me!"

"That's because he never has any," P.J. muttered to Morgan. "I'll be secretary again. I like taking the minutes. I could be advertising manager, too, I guess. Would the advertising manager be the one to make the signs? I make terrific signs!"

"I could be sales manager," Mikey offered. "What does a sales manager do, Morg?"

"Takes care of sales. What else? He could also be in charge of the inventory, seeing it all gets priced and tagged and listed in an inventory book. Every time anything gets traded in or out, we have to make a note of it in the inventory book. My dad says that's real important on account of shoplifters."

"Shoplifters?" Mikey breathed, and he looked kind of shocked. "Gee, I never thought about shoplifters. It's not all fun and games being in business, you know it?"

"Who's gonna be prezdent?" Sanford kept shouting at them. Morgan played it cool. He acted as if the idea of being president hadn't even occurred to him.

"Since we all seem to be keeping the same jobs, I think it ought to be Morgan," P.J. declared. "The idea for a kids' trading company was his to begin with, and he's the best one at running things and being in charge."

"At figuring things out and talking to people also," Mikey added.

"Why don't you guys marry him if you love him so much?" Fergy gave Morgan a resentful look, produced a banana out of thin air, and started eating it.

"Banana," Sanford said in his Magilla Gorilla voice. "Gimme banana *now!*" He made a grab for it. Fergy held it over his head so he couldn't reach it. As soon as Sanford backed off, he gobbled the whole thing up in three gulps.

"Boy, some people are soooo greedy," Sanford remarked, and resumed trotting.

"I make a motion that Morgan be president," P.J. said, and stuck her tongue out at Fergy.

"I second the motion," Mikey chimed in.

"I third it," Sanford added. The he smiled sweetly at them and cooed, "So, now what's my job gonna be, I wonder?"

"You're just an honorary Turtle," Morgan said to him, "so you don't get a job. Not yet, anyway. When you become a full-fledged Turtle, then you'll get a job, Sanford."

"But when will I become a full-fledged Turtle, Morgan?"

Morgan grinned at the others. "When you have earned it, Sanford, old boy."

"But when will that be?"

"When you have made some real contribution to the club and earned the right to call yourself a Turtle. Now cool it, Sanford. We Turtles have a lot of important things to discuss, and we don't want you interrupting us with all this trivial stuff."

"What's more important than me bein' a Turtle?" Sanford whispered to himself. Then he rammed his thumb in his mouth and started sucking away.

"Back to the question of how much commission we ought to charge," Morgan went on. "I've been giving the matter a lot of thought, and I still feel it ought to be no more than ten percent. That seems fair."

"Fair to who, the customers? It's certainly not fair to us," Fergy muttered. P.J. said he was just being greedy and money-hungry. They started arguing back and forth, getting nowhere fast. Finally, out of exasperation, they decided to put it to a vote. It was two in favor of charging ten percent, one against, and one abstaining.

Morgan looked at Mikey. He knew how Mikey felt, but this was a crucial decision. The whole future of their business could depend on it. His vote could make the difference. "You do have an opinion, don't you, Mikey?" he asked.

Mikey nodded. "I don't want to make anybody mad at me, though."

"Mikey, when it comes to taking a stand—expressing an opinion on an important issue like this—and making a major contribution to the club, you can't worry about whether somebody is going to be mad at you or not. You have to forget about that and say how you feel. You owe it to the rest of us."

Mikey's consciousness got raised by what Morgan said. He was inspired. "I vote for charging ten percent!" he exclaimed, and flung his arm up in the air.

Fergy shot Morgan an evil look. "He'll say anything he thinks you want him to say. I hope you realize what this means, Pierpont. It means so long, Turtle Street Trading Company, that's what it means!

8

Problems...

hey decided to have the grand opening the next week, on Saturday, July 21. Business hours would be from ten to six instead of nine to five in order to give them some extra time to get things set up. There was still a lot to do, but they had to open as soon as possible. It was the middle of July right now. In a little over two weeks it would be August, then September, and then school would start.

"Will we still be in business after that?" Mikey asked.

"Sure, but only on weekends," Morgan replied. "Well, fellow Turtles, I guess that just about covers everything."

"Except for one minor item," P.J. said. "How we're going to get all our stuff back and forth to that parking lot every day, or are you planning to travel on wings of song?"

"I never thought of that," Morgan groaned. How could he have overlooked something as crucial as transportation? They discussed the situation. As usual nobody was willing to ask his parents, so he wound up asking *his*. He promised himself he wouldn't, but it was either that or scrap the business. Anything was preferable to that.

His parents conferred and came up with a counter offer, one he was in no position to refuse. They would take turns providing transportation to and from the parking lot if, and only if, Morgan and Sanford would agree to take on some extra chores around the house. Morgan agreed without even bothering to consult with Sanford. If the kid really wanted to be a part of the business, and especially if he was going to get a share of the earnings, he would have to start to pull his own weight.

That afternoon Morgan biked down to *The Pennysaver*'s offices on Ventura Boulevard to place the ad announcing their grand opening. They had already spent $21.85 of Felicia's twenty-five dollars on supplies. That left $3.15, plus the seventy-eight cents Morgan still had left from his allowance. The ad would cost $3.70. Out of their total assets, that would leave them twenty-three cents.

Morgan had written the ad in his notebook. It was a good ad, if he did say so himself. It did everything a good ad was supposed to do: It provided all the pertinent information in an interesting way, and it was short, sweet, and to the point:

> *Kids! Bring all your old junk and trade it at the grand opening of the TURTLE STREET TRADING COMPANY, the Turtles' answer to being rich, in the parking lot outside of Ralph's in the Mulview Shopping Center at Mulwood & San Luis roads, Calabasas, on July 21 from 10 a.m. to 6 p.m. and on Sunday, July 22, same hours. Free prizes, free refreshments, and a famous secret celebrity to sign autographs.*

It made Morgan feel that he really was a bona fide business owner to walk into *The Pennysaver*'s office, put his money and the ad on the countertop, and say to the teen-aged boy behind the counter in his most grown-up voice, "I want to place an ad in this week's issue of your publication, please." The older boy seemed impressed. When he read over the ad Morgan had written, he was even more impressed.

"Great idea for a business!" he said. "Sounds like it can't miss."

"I hope you're right," Morgan replied self-importantly. "I just want to make sure the ad will appear in this week's issue. With our big grand opening coming up on Saturday, we can't afford to have any slipups. No ad, no customers, if you get my drift."

"Oh, don't worry," the boy assured him. "It will be in, and I'll make sure it's very noticeable."

"That's nice of you. Thanks!" Morgan said, heading for the door.

"Lots of luck!" the boy called after him.

Morgan was excited. That ad would reach thousands of people all over the area, not only in Calabasas, but also in all the neighboring communities. Even if the kids themselves didn't read it, their parents would and, hopefully, would tell them about it. Customers would come flocking. There was no doubt in Morgan's mind that the grand opening of the Turtle Street Trading Company was going to be a huge success.

P.J. had swallowed her pride and asked her stepfather, who owned a toy store in Chatsworth, if he would donate some things they could give away as free prizes. For refreshments they were going to serve fruit punch, graciously donated by Morgan's mom. Morgan had planned on asking Glenn Nakku, a boy from his school who was a state skateboard champion, to be their secret celebrity, but Mr. Weintraub had come up with a much better idea. He was good friends with Tommy Tracer, singing cowboy of stage, screen, and TV. He said he was sure, if he asked him very nicely, that Tommy Tracer would agree to be their secret celebrity for the day. Morgan was only afraid that, in return for putting in a personal appearance on their behalf, he would expect some financial compensation, but Mr. Weintraub assured him that ol' Tommy would be plumb proud to do it for free, 'cause any friends of Freddie Weintraub's were jes' naturally friends of his too.

9

...and More
Problems

They were at Mikey's making the signs when P.J. dropped the bomb on them.

"My mother says she won't let me be in the business if I don't do what she says."

Morgan, Mikey, and Fergy all looked at one another. They didn't have to ask her what she meant. They already knew. P.J. was being blackmailed by her own mother. Her mother wasn't going to let her be in the business unless she promised to stop wearing her cowboy clothes and put on a dress, comb her hair, take more baths, wear girly shoes instead of cowboy boots, clean up her room, clean up her act, and generally stop being so moody and difficult to get along with. Maybe she was even going to insist that P.J. go back to her ballet lessons.

"What are you going to do?" Morgan asked. He wondered if even the business was worth a sacrifice like that on P.J.'s part.

She shrugged and muttered, "I don't know. What do you think I should do?"

"Don't ask me! I'm just an innocent bystander." Morgan couldn't figure it out. Okay, so P.J.'s mom wasn't all that crazy about having a cowperson for a daughter, but P.J. was P.J., and she was great the way she was. Besides, there was no way you were going to change her, so it was useless to try. Anyway, didn't her mother know there had to be all kinds of people in this world? Different people had different ideas and wanted different things. That's what made them so interesting. Not every girl in creation wanted to grow up to be a ballerina.

Morgan knew that he couldn't make a decision like that for someone else. P.J. would have to work it out for herself. It would break his heart if she couldn't be with them, but that was up to her.

Obviously Fergy didn't think so. "How can you be so selfish?" he said to her. "Don't you care about the rest of us? Big deal! So you put on a dress for once. It's not going to kill you, is it?"

P.J. didn't respond. She didn't have to. You knew she was thinking it just might.

The signs were all finished by one o'clock. Except for Sanford, who had an appointment with his allergy doctor, they all took off in different directions to put them up. They had made fifty signs altogether. They were going to be posted on telephone poles and around shopping centers all up and down Ventura Boulevard between here and Encino, and in three of the local malls too. Morgan was going to put one up at the Topanga Mall right near the Orange Julius stand. That was a very strategic location. Sooner or later every kid in the valley showed up there.

By the time he'd finished putting up his twelve signs, he was exhausted. He couldn't wait to get home, have a cold drink, then jump in the kiddie pool. But he knew his duty. He had to stop at Mikey's and check in first.

"Turtletaub!" he gasped when he staggered into Mikey's garage. He didn't even bother to make the secret signal. At a time like this just the password would have to do. He collapsed on the floor and lay there panting. He wasn't the only one. P.J. was stretched out on her back with her eyes closed and her hands folded over her chest. Morgan thought she looked like a corpse, and told her so.

"I *am* one," she said. "I died around Petunia Street on the way back from Encino. It was a hundred and two, and I didn't even have fifty cents for a soda."

"Ever hear of water? That's free!" Fergy lifted his head long enough to smirk at her. He, too, was stretched out on the floor with his tennis shoes off and his bare feet propped up on Mr. McGrath's workbench, guzzling soda pop and recuperating from his difficult ordeal.

Mikey was lying draped over a packing case. "I like hot weather," he informed them. "It always reminds me of that great trip my dad and I made to Big Bend State Park in Texas when it was a hundred and twenty in the shade—only there wasn't any shade—and the Grande River turned into cracked mud."

Sanford came in. "Doctor Mellon gave me two 'jections," he declared in a complaining tone. "And they hurt!"

Morgan hardly heard him. He was too busy staring at P.J. She looked different today, but he couldn't figure out why. Maybe it was because she wasn't wearing her hat?

Who could possibly stand to wear a hat on a hot day like this? All of a sudden it hit him. It wasn't just the hat that was missing. It was the rest of her John Wayne suit, too. *Zounds!* he thought, and his eyes opened wide. P.J. was wearing a dress, a blue one with puffed sleeves and a sash around the waist. She looked like Alice in Wonderland after she'd drunk the potion that made her grow taller.

She saw Morgan staring at her and snapped, "What's the matter? Haven't you ever seen a girl in a dress before?"

Fergy looked at her and said, "Girl? What girl? I don't see any girl. Just a boy wearing a dress!"

That made P.J. so furious, she forgot she was dead. She jumped up and started storming around the garage screaming at Fergy, calling him all sorts of terrifically original and imaginative names, like Fat Fergy, Fergus the Fat, Ferguson Fattraub, Gargantua, and that old standby, Hippo Boy.

Sanford decided to take that inopportune moment to start in on one of his favorite Fifties songs, "Devil with the Blue Dress On."

Fergy added fuel to the fire by saying in the high voice of a girl, "Oooh, prissy Miss Priscilla Jane, what a sweet wittle gir-wums!"

All anybody had to do to drive P.J. up the nearest wall was call her Priscilla Jane. It wasn't exactly the most appropriate name for a girl who thought she was John Wayne. Morgan couldn't blame her for having a tantrum—which she did in short order.

"Good golly, Miss Molly!" Sanford sang, launching into the next offering in his Fifties medley.

Morgan gave it two more seconds, then intervened. At this point in the proceedings, friction in the ranks was the last thing they needed.

"Cut it out, you guys. You're in direct violation of Bylaw Number Two: 'No Turtle will knowingly, and with malice aforethought, pick a fight with a fellow Turtle, even under extreme duress.'"

P.J. stormed off muttering to herself about Fergy's being the extremest duress imaginable. Fergy headed for Fallon's Ice Cream Parlor to get a double Pig Trough, which was free to anyone disgusting enough to eat it all up in one sitting. Morgan, Mikey, and Sanford headed for the kiddie pool in Morgan's backyard.

"That was noble of P.J., sacrificing herself for the common cause that way," Morgan said as they were heading down Turtle Street in the midafternoon heat. "Considering the circumstances, I thought that was a pretty low blow on Fergy's part. A close call, too, I might add. Another couple of minutes and, if I hadn't intervened, we might have been having a funeral instead of a grand opening."

"We still might," Mikey intoned in a creepy voice like Dracula's. "Remember, fellow Transylvanians, today is Friday the thirteenth!"

10

A Not So
Grand Opening

Morgan wasn't the least bit superstitious, but he kept his fingers crossed just in case. Luckily they got through the rest of the afternoon without any mishaps.

They all took the next day off to rest up. It was going to be a busy week, and besides, it was Saturday, and on Saturdays Morgan and Sanford usually went to the store with their dad to help out. Morgan wondered how he was going to manage without them when, starting next Saturday, they had their own business to run and wouldn't be available to help him with his.

The rest of the week it was work, work, and more work. The Turtles were busy every minute.

"If you think this is busy, wait till we open. Then you'll find out what busy is!" Morgan said to the others as they were pricing the last of the inventory on Friday night.

He was too excited to sleep. How could he sleep when the business was going to open in a few hours? He got up at sunrise and went outside to see what the weather was like. Just what he had been afraid of. It was going to be another hot day. Six A.M. and eighty degrees already. At that rate it would probably be a hundred and six by noontime. On such a hot day would people want to leave their nice, cool, air-conditioned houses and come hang around a sizzling parking lot, or would they go to the beach instead?

He couldn't help worrying. So many things could still go wrong. What if they didn't get one customer the whole day? What if they didn't make any money and couldn't pay back the loan? What if it got so hot that everyone passed out from heat prostration? What if the tar on the parking lot melted? What if Mr. Weintraub had forgotten to ask Tommy Tracer, or he didn't show up? What if . . . ?

In the middle of one of Morgan's more disastrous *what if*'s, Fergy, Mikey, and P.J. appeared. P.J. looked more like a cheerleader than a cowperson in her white shorts, a bright pink tank top, and matching pink tennis shoes. Her hair was in bunches, tied with pink ribbons. Her face was the exact same shade of pink.

"My mother said I couldn't come unless I wore *this*," she explained, gesturing to her outfit. The shorts made her legs look even longer and skinnier than they were.

By the time they got to the parking lot it was nine o'clock, and Morgan's stomach felt like Ventura Boulevard during rush hour. Sanford had insisted on bringing Snooky and the kittens. He was carrying them around in a tomato soup carton, and he had found an old beach umbrella in Mikey's garage to put over them to keep them cool.

Mrs. McGrath and Morgan and P.J.'s moms were already at the shopping center setting things up. They had volunteered to help. The table was set up on the grass, and it had a pretty paper tablecloth on it. The cartons were lined up underneath it. There was the big one with the free prizes in it plus the six inventory cartons, each marked with how much all the items in it were worth. The first was marked 10¢ to 25¢; the second, 25¢; the third, 50¢; the fourth, $1.00; the fifth, $1.50 to $2.00; and the sixth, $2.50 to $5.00.

P.J.'s sign was propped up in front of the table. It had the company name in big purple letters. Underneath that was a fat turtle wearing a Turtles T-shirt and tennis shoes.

Morgan was keeping one eye peeled for Mr. Weintraub. "I just hope he'll show up," he said to Fergy.

"Don't worry," Fergy replied. "My dad's flaky, he's not that flaky." Famous last words! At a little before ten the red pickup pulled in and skidded to a screeching stop at the table. Mr. Weintraub climbed out. Morgan looked inside the truck. The only one in there was Aloysius Q. Weintraub, Fergy's mixed-breed hound.

"Where's Mr. Tracer?" Morgan asked in a voice he knew sounded pretty hysterical.

"He'll be here," Mr. Weintraub replied in that easygoing drawl of his. "He had to stop and pick up a friend first."

"A girl friend?" P.J. squealed. According to *People* magazine, Tommy Tracer and Cissy Manteen, stars of the new TV series *Fortune's Folly*, were going together.

"I reckon you could say that," Mr. Weintraub drawled lackadaisically, leaving them every bit as uninformed as they had been a moment before.

"Here come your first customers now, Turtles," Morgan's dad said as a station wagon pulled up and a bunch of little kids tumbled out, all climbing over one another to get to the table and be first on line. There were six of them, and they all looked exactly alike.

Morgan donned his businessperson smile. "No pushing. Everybody line up. You'll all get a turn. What can I do for you?" he asked the little girl in the denim overalls.

She shoved a baby doll at him and replied, "I want to trade my dolly!"

"You do? Okay, just let me see it." He looked it over. It was bald, and there was a crack in one of its arms, but aside from that it was in pretty good condition. He figured it was worth a dollar and no more, so he said, "Your dolly is worth a dollar, little girl. That means you can trade it for anything you like in that carton, the one marked one dollar."

She stared at him for a second. Then she yelled, "I want my mommy!" and ran back to the car.

The next kid stuck a stuffed animal under Morgan's nose and informed him, "I brought Snoopy!"

"Oh, that's nice. He's real cute, but the little girl was here first, so you'll have to wait, okay?"

The little girl was coming back, and she had her mother with her. Morgan clutched. The mother didn't look too friendly.

"What kind of operation are you running here, young man?"

Morgan gelt his smile slipping. One minute in business, and already he had an irate customer on his hands!

"That doll's worth much more than a dollar," the little girl's mother went on.

Morgan retrieved the smile and said meekly, "Oh, it's really a very nice doll, ma'am, but, as you can plainly see, it is kind of bald, and it has a crack in one arm."

"Where? Show me a crack! I don't see any crack."

"Right here, ma'am," Morgan said, and pointed to the crack. He didn't want to be disrespectful or anything, but if she couldn't see it, she must be blind. "If you'll just allow me to explain how our service works," he went on, "I'm sure you'll see we're not trying to take advantage of anyone. Every item in our inventory is marked with a price. It's all divided into separate cartons, and all the cartons are marked with the prices of the items in them.

"When a customer brings something in, he—or she in this case—wants to trade, we check it out and give it a fair price, depending on what shape it's in and what it cost when it was new. Based on the condition it is in, I feel that a dollar is a fair value to put on your little girl's dolly, which means that she's entitled to trade it for anything in our inventory worth one dollar. If she'll go and look through the contents of that carton over there, the one marked one dollar, I'm sure she'll find something she'd like to trade it for. But just in case she doesn't, tell you what I'll do. I'll let her select something from the two-dollar carton instead."

"Just why should you do that?" the woman inquired suspiciously, and looked him up and down.

Morgan felt slightly dishonest. "Well, for one thing, because you're our first customer of the day, ma'am. And, for another, I'm anxious to please you and make you happy so you'll come back again. See, satisfied customers come back. Unsatisfied ones don't."

"And just what do you kids get out of all this, aside from the joy of having a satisfied customer?"

Morgan glanced around. He was pretty embarrassed. Everybody was listening, waiting with bated breath to hear what he would say and how he was going to handle the situation. He felt the way he always did at school just before taking an important test, a hard one with lots of complicated questions on it, only on this test anything less than an A plus was failing. "Well, here goes," he thought, and summoned up all his courage.

"Ma'am, we're running a strictly legitimate operation here, but we're not in it for fun or charity. We'd like to come out making a little money—just enough to cover our overhead expenses and repay us, in some small part, for all the time and effort we've put in. We feel we're providing a pretty unique service to the public, one no one has provided before, while promoting a less wasteful attitude on the part of today's youth."

She burst out laughing. He felt like a fool. "Young man, you're very gifted. That speech was positively inspiring!" she said, and grabbed the little girl's hand. "All right, we're going to look though this carton and find ourselves a nice toy to trade our dolly in for, aren't we, sweetheart?"

"Yes, Mommy," the little girl chirped, and started pulling everything out of the carton and throwing it around, and making a big mess.

"By the way," the mother said to Morgan. "For your information Desmond is a little boy, not a little girl. Aren't you, Desmond?"

Morgan thought he would die, but how could he have known? All little kids that age looked pretty much alike, especially in overalls; especially if they had never had a haircut in their natural lives.

Desmond had found a stuffed elephant in the dollar carton. He picked it up and kissed it. His mother came over and said, "How much do I owe you, young man?"

Morgan flashed his ivories. "Just a mere ten cents, ma'am, our commission on the transaction."

She slapped a dime on the table. "It was worth it just to see you in action," she said with a smile. She started to drag Desmond to the car. The other kids ran after her, and she herded them all into the back. Through the rear window Desmond made his elephant wave bye-bye to Morgan.

"Good-bye, young man," his mother called out the car window as she pulled away. "Good luck in your new business. Not that I think you'll need luck, a smart, super salesperson like you!"

Morgan grinned at his fellow Turtles. "Maybe we ought to have this framed," he said, and held up the dime. It glinted and gleamed in the sunlight. Boy, it looked beautiful! "The first money we've made in our new business."

11

Scratch One Business!

Morgan dropped the dime in the cash box and glanced at his watch. Eleven o'clock already? Time flew when you were having fun! Desmond & Friend had taken up a lot of time. The Turtles would have to be speedier if they wanted to make money.

"Here. You earned this," P.J. said, and handed Morgan a cup of punch. He drank it in a single gulp and held the cup out for a refill. It was hot all right, and getting hotter every second. Heat waves were shimmering in the air above the asphalt, and the tar was melting in gooey patches.

For the next two hours the few people who came to the shopping center went to Ralph's or the cleaner's or one of the other stores. Nobody was beating a path to the Turtle Street Trading Company.

"On weekends people sleep late," his dad said by way of explanation.

Morgan shrugged. "Yeah, and then they go to the beach!" Maybe he was just thinking negatively, but he had a funny sensation in his stomach. Either it was the punch, or his sixth sense was telling him something, like his *what if*'s hadn't been so farfetched after all.

Twelve o'clock and sweltering, and still no customers. No Tommy Tracer, either, which just went to prove that Mr. Weintraub *was* that flaky.

At a little after one o'clock a vintage Mustang pulled up. A horde of teen-agers piled out, and the Turtles made a grand total of two dollars trading posters and T-shirts. Morgan was waiting on a kid who had brought in a bunch of records he wanted to trade in for some cassette tapes. All of a sudden Mikey let out a yell.

"Everybody, *look!*"

Galloping into the parking lot was a magnificent white horse, and on its back sat none other than Tommy Tracer in person. He looked like the Mr. Clean of the cowboy world in his white cowboy suit, white Stetson hat, white cowboy boots, and belt, gun holsters, and six-shooters. Even his saddle was white. So was the guitar slung across his back.

The horse pranced and danced across the parking lot, doing tricks and showing off for the people. It pawed the ground, tossed its braided mane, and snorted. It reared up on its hind legs and whinnied. It was some spirited horse! Tommy whipped off his hat and waved it around and around over his head. You expected him to whip out those six-guns, too, and start shooting the place up the way he did in those cowboy movies. He tugged on the reins, and his horse started sidestepping sedately toward them like a trick horse in the circus, the kind the bareback riders rode. It looked pretty pleased with itself.

"What a horse!" P.J. breathed, and you could tell she was thinking that after seeing this one, True Grit really did seem like a nag.

"So that's the friend Mr. Weintraub said Tommy had to pick up on his way here," Morgan murmured.

Tommy rode up to the table. "Howdy, Turtles. Nice day!"

"It is now that you're here, Mr. Tracer," Morgan said. "We Turtles can't thank you enough. It's awfully nice of you to do this for us."

"Don't mention it, kid," Tommy drawled. "Tex and I are plumb proud to do it, ain't we, Tex?"

Morgan couldn't believe it. The horse whinnied right on cue the minute he said that, just as though it understood.

"Lahk I said to ol' Freddie jes' the other day," Tommy went on. "Any friends of his is jes' natchrelly friends of ol' Tommy's too!"

Tommy Tracer hung around for a while talking to them. A few people came over, and he signed autographs for them. P.J. and the horse went off by themselves to get acquainted. By the time Tommy rode off into the sunset, they had become pretty intimate.

When Tommy rode off, so did everybody else in the parking lot. By three o'clock it was a ghost town, hotter than Death Valley in August.

"Scratch one business!" Fergy muttered, and went to Fallon's to gorge himself again. Morgan was down in the dumps. This was too depressing for words. Fergy was right. The business was a colossal failure. They might as well pack it in.

But Morgan's father didn't seem to think it was a failure at all. The way he acted, you'd have thought their grand opening had been a huge success.

"Son, that idea of yours is a real winner," he said when they got home. "In fact, it's even better than I thought it was."

Morgan couldn't believe his dad was saying that. "Come on, Dad. You can't con me. You and I both know it ought to win first prize in the Businesses That Never Got Off the Ground Contest."

"No, son. The idea is terrific. Your only problem is the amount of commission you're charging. I knew from the start ten percent wasn't enough."

"You did? How come you didn't say anything to me, Dad?"

"You wanted to do this all by yourself, son, so I decided to let you. After all, that's the only way you learn, by making your own mistakes, then correcting them. That's how I learned when I went into business."

"Wasn't Pierpont's Party Supply an overnight success?" Morgan asked, kind of amazed.

His father shook his head. "It was weeks before I took in a penny in profit, and I had a lot more at stake than you kids—a family to support, a lot of overhead expenses to pay, and don't forget rent on the store. Believe me, I was plenty scared. I even thought of packing it in, but I didn't. And in the end, when my business turned out to be a big success, I was awfully glad."

"My dad says we ought to hang in. Once word gets around, the business will start to take off," Morgan said to the others when they met at Mikey's garage for an emergency meeting that night. "He says our one mistake was not charging enough commission." He looked at Fergy. "I was wrong. You were right, Ferg. What do we do about it? We made a mistake, sure, but we can correct it by charging more starting tomorrow."

"Big of you to admit you were wrong, Pierpont," Fergy said. "Not everyone can do that. I admire you for being able to."

"Thanks, Weintraub," Morgan replied, really flattered by Fergy's compliment.

"I don't know," P.J. mused. "What'll the customers think if we start charging twenty or twenty-five percent after charging only ten?"

"They'll think we got smart all of a sudden," Fergy told her.

"Anyway, aside from Desmond & Friend, we didn't have that many customers," Morgan added. "No one will know the difference, unless Desmond's mommy decides to come to the parking lot and make an announcement. If we keep on charging only ten, we'll be out of business by tomorrow night—which may happen anyway."

"If we are, we can't go to Disneyland," Sanford said. "I make a movement we charge twenty-five percent! "

"Motion, not movement, Sandy," P.J. told him.

"Okay, motion. Somebody second my motion, quick," Sanford bellowed at them. When no one did, he seconded it himself.

Morgan asked for a show of hands. It was unanimous in favor of raising the commission to twenty-five percent as of first thing tomorrow morning. Morgan just hoped they would get some customers. If as few came as today, it wouldn't matter how much they charged. They'd be out of business by tomorrow night anyway. He acted confident in front of the others, but deep down inside he was anything but.

12

A Full-fledged Turtle

All Morgan could say was the next time he came up with a brainstorm, he planned on ignoring it!

When he got home he went upstairs, washed his hands and face, brushed his teeth, got into his pajamas, and climbed into bed. At this point he was even too tired to feel depressed. "Sleep, glorious sleep!" he thought as he snuggled down under the covers.

But old Sanford had other ideas. Standing on tiptoe putting something away in the dresser, he started singing at the top of his lungs.

"Loo-see in the sky-yi with die-monds!"

He wasn't exactly Paul McCartney. Morgan rolled over and said, "Shut up, will you, Sanford? I'm trying to sleep."

Sanford didn't much care whether Morgan got to sleep or not. He kept right on singing just to be annoying. There was something on Morgan's mind, something he had been wanting to say to Sanford all day, but he was having a little problem getting it out. Sanford just wasn't the type you said things like this to; not if you could help it, anyway. He pulled the quilt up to his chin, turned over on the other side, and cleared his throat a couple of times loudly.

"*Ahem! Hrrumph!* Sanford, you did a good job today. On behalf of all the Turtles, I thank you!" he said very quickly.

Sanford came over and stood beside Morgan's bed. Morgan thought he was about to say something truly inspiring, but he ruined the whole thing by saying something truly stupid instead. "I was terrific, wasn't I? Did you see the way I handled that bratty Amy Neilson? She was bein' so 'noxious, but I knew 'xactly what to do. I just went out of my way to be extra nice to her, and that way she wound up tradin' a whole buncha super stuff."

Morgan didn't say anything. He didn't want to bust Sanford's toy balloon, but if you happened to know Amy Neilson, you knew she couldn't be bratty or obnoxious if she tried. She was just too good a kid.

Obviously Sanford thought one day on the job earned him the right to become a Turtle. "Can I be a full-flegged Turtle now, Morg?"

Morgan sighed wearily. "Fledged, not flegged, Sanford. And no, you can't!"

"How come?"

"I can't decide a thing like that all by myself. I have to consult with the other Turtles. We have to nominate you for membership and then take a vote. If the vote's three out of four in favor of you becoming a Turtle, you're a Turtle, but if it's *not*, then tough luck on *you*, Sanford Ronald. Turtledom is still in your far-distant future!"

Sanford didn't like that one bit. He started stamping his foot and shouting in Morgan's ear. "Unfair! Unfair! Unfair!" All of a sudden his face went white, and he stopped shouting and started sneezing instead.

"Ah-choooo!"

He sneezed once, the loudest sneeze in the history of the world. Then he went ahead and sneezed twice more. *"Ah-choo! Ah-choo!"*

Three was the magic number. When Sanford sneezed once, you ignored it. When he sneezed twice, you paid attention. When he sneezed three times in a row like that, you got up and made a mad dash for the nasal spray and the tissues, because that could mean he was about to have one of his famous allergy attacks.

"Sanford, don't move. Don't panic, and for gosh sakes, *don't sneeze*. I'll be right back." Morgan flew down the hall to the bathroom and came back with Sanford's atomizer. He gave each of Sanford's nostrils two good squirts and handed him a tissue.

Sanford blew his nose. He wiggled it at Morgan and said, "Itchy!" He didn't sneeze, at least not right then. He said he was going to, though.

"I'b godda steeze againd, Borgand."

Morgan waited with bated breath, atomizer and tissues ready, but Sanford didn't sneeze. They looked at one another. "Well? Morgan said. "Are you or aren't you?"

Sanford shrugged. "I aren't. False alarb, Borgand," he added, and padded over to his bed. "You cand go to bed dnow."

Morgan waited an extra minute just to be on the safe side. You never knew when another sneeze might be forthcoming.

Sanford poked his nose out of the covers and said, "I'b okay, Borgand. Honest. Go to bed dnow." You're a good brotherb."

Morgan climbed back into bed. He slid down under the covers and closed his eyes. It was peaceful and quiet now. The only sounds in the room were an occasional sniffle from the other bed and the steady ticking of the clock on the dresser. He could feel himself drifting off to Never Neverland...

"Borgand?"

"*Uh?* Wha...wha. What, Sanford?"

"You asleep?"

"Yeah! Can't you hear me snoring?"

"I did a real good job today, didn't I?"

"I said so, didn't I? What do you want, a medal?"

"No, just to be a full-flegged Turtle, Borgand."

Morgan groaned. What was the use? One way or the other, the little creep always got his way in the end, so why fight it?

"Okay, Sanford, you win. I'll talk to the other Turtles. I'll put in a good word for you. We'll take a vote. Now good night!"

Morgan closed his eyes. Just before he drifted off to Never Neverland he heard his little brother whisper, "Boy, a full-flegged Turtle. Now, if I could only have a kitten, I'd be the happiest kid in the world!"

13

A Little Help from a Friend

Sanford climbed out of the back of the station wagon. He grabbed the tomato soup carton and, stepping very carefully, carried it over to the grass island and set it down underneath the tree. He went back and got the umbrella and stuck it in the grass alongside it so that it shaded the carton from the blazing sun.

"Don't you worry about a thing," he said to Snooky, who was looking up at him worshipfully. "I won't let anybody bother you and your babies. Your Sandy's here to watch over you and protect you."

Morgan helped Mikey unload a carton. "Like my dad says, once word gets around, the customers will start coming, but it could take weeks and weeks."

"Weeks? We'll be back in school by then," Mikey said. He made it sound like a fate worse than death.

Fergy helped P.J. with a carton. "We can't wait weeks. *I* can't, anyway." He grunted, and proceeded to drop his end on her foot.

"*Ouch!* Clumsy oaf, you just broke my toe." She carried the carton the rest of the way by herself. "I still say it's dumb to stay in a business that isn't making money. How do we know the customers will ever come? Who wants to hang around here getting sunstroke if we're never going to make any money?"

Morgan's dad smiled and said, "Think positive, Turtles! Tell yourselves you're going to be successful, and you *will* be."

"Maybe we ought to wish on a star and ask Jiminy Cricket for help too," P.J. muttered. Mr. Pierpont just laughed.

Off in a world of his own, Sanford was acting out one of his favorite scenes from *Star Wars*, the intergalactic battle with the laser swords, only he was rewriting the dialogue in his own words: "Die, earthling earthworm!" he said in an ominous, gravelly voice that was supposed to be Darth Vader but sounded a lot like their Aunt Charlotte instead.

When their dad called to him, he replayed the scene backward, doing everything in reverse down to the last sword thrust and parry.

"Sanford, you belong in the movies," their dad said, and hugged the little nut. He hugged Morgan, too, and then got behind the wheel of the wagon. "Think positive!" they heard him call, his voice wafting back to them as he drove away.

"Easy for him to say," Fergy grumbled. "He's got a thriving business already. He's going there to make money. We're staying here to die of sunstroke."

"Now you sound like P.J.," Morgan said accusingly. "P.J. the pessimist. Whatever happened to 'Think positive'?"

"Look, everybody, I'm thinking positive!" P.J. leered at them. She had small eyes and practically no nose whatsoever. When she leered, her eyes disappeared in a mass of crinkles, her nose got swallowed up by her cheeks, and all you saw were lots of pearly white teeth.

"Keep smiling. Here come some customers," Morgan said to her as three kids came strolling across the parking lot. They strolled right on past and went to Fallon's Ice Cream Parlor. A few more kids came, but they came only to look, not trade. Nobody else showed up until after eleven, at which point they got two customers, one who traded something and another who stood around sneering and making derogatory remarks about the business. Morgan wanted to punch him right in the mouth, but he remembered what his dad was always saying—"The customer is always right!"—and controlled the impulse.

"Let's close up and go get some lunch," Fergy suggested a little before noon.

"Can't. No money," Morgan informed him.

85

"What? No lunch money?" Mikey cried in a shocked voice. He was convinced that if they skipped a meal, they'd all have malnutrition by dinnertime.

"Why don't we give all this junk away and go home?" Fergy said. He was in the world's worst mood.

"We can't go home," Morgan reminded him. "We said we'd be open all day. What if customers come and we're not here?"

"They'll go home. Am I supposed to starve to death while we're at it?"

Morgan jingled the change in his pocket. He had exactly forty cents. He pulled it out and handed it to Fergy. "Here! Go stuff yourself."

"Thanks!" Fergy stared at the coins in his palm. "What am I supposed to buy with this? One prune?"

"It's all I've got. Take it or leave it. On second thought, give me back a dime. I have to make a phone call."

He headed for Ralph's and the pay phone. He just hoped his mom was home and that, if she *was*, she wouldn't get mad if he asked her to bring them down something to eat.

"I don't suppose you'd consider extending a little credit to five starving fellow businesspersons," he quipped, making a little joke as he passed the manager's booth.

"You kids not makin' any money yet?" Mr. Frank asked.

"Yet? You mean *never*," Morgan replied.

"Business a little slow? Funny, I thought you'd make out just fine. Could be the heat, I guess. Could be word hasn't gotten 'round 'bout you yet; but mark my words, young fellow, once it *does*, customers'll come arunnin'. Like I said to your dad, that's some right smart idea you kids have got there!"

"You really think so, Mr. Frank?"

"Wouldn't say so if I didn't think so, Morgan."

"Gee, thanks! That makes me feel a whole lot better." If Mr. Frank thought it was a good idea, maybe it was. Mr. Frank took out his wallet and started peeling off one-dollar bills. "Oh, no. Gosh, Mr. Frank, that was supposed to be a joke. I didn't mean it when I asked you for money."

"When you get on your feet, you'll pay it back," Mr. Frank said, and handed him ten one-dollar bills.

Morgan was really moved by his display of confidence and trust. "I'll never forget you for this, Mr. Frank!" he exclaimed as he headed for the dairy case.

When Mikey saw the big bag of groceries, he got scared. "Did you do what I think you did, Morgan?"

"Yeah. Just call me Sticky Fingers Pierpont!" Morgan started to unpack the groceries. "Let's see, what have we got here? Cheese, crackers, milk, bananas, apples, pears, dried fruit, cookies . . ."

"Cookies?" Fergy grabbed the box of peanut butter

cookies and ran off to eat it by himself. Mikey was watching Morgan, a horrified look in his eyes. He kept glancing furtively around to see whether the entire Los Angeles Police Department would descend on the parking lot, sirens screaming. It would be curtains for the Turtle Gang.

P.J. took an apple and some cheese and sat down on the curb to eat them. She stretched out her long legs and said, "Boy, am I tired! My legs are killing me."

"I can understand why in those boots," Morgan remarked. He helped himself to a pear and went over and leaned against a Camaro that was parked nearby.

"Cock a doodle doo! *I'm* Rooster Cogburn," Sanford crowed, and started running around in little circles, flapping his arms like a rooster having a tantrum. "The Duke had a pair of cowboy boots 'xactly like that in *Too Grit*," he told P.J.

"*True*, not *too*, Sandy," she said, and took a bite of apple. "In *True Grit* he played Rooster Cogburn for the first time."

"You mean he played him more'n oncet?"

"Twice. Once in *True Grit* and again in *Rooster Cogburn*, with Katharine Hepburn."

"*Huh*?" Sanford looked a little confused.

"*Rooster Cogburn* was the name of the movie, too, Sandy," P.J. explained. Just then a van pulled in, and she said, "Wow, what a beauty! I'm going to have one just like that someday, when I get my horse ranch in Arizona."

"I won't hold my breath," Fergy called over.

Mikey whispered to Morgan, "What's with Fergy? He sure is acting mean!"

Morgan shrugged and replied, "No meaner than usual."

14

Disneyland, Here We Come!

That van really was a beauty. Somebody had done an airbrush painting of a desert scene on it. It was so realistic, you almost thought you were there in the sand dunes, the cactus in bloom, the coyotes howling.

Morgan was still lounging against the Camaro, but now he was daydreaming about drifting desert sands, so he didn't notice that the van was heading straight for him until it was about to run him over. He leaped onto the hood of the Camaro just in time and started yelling his head off. The door of the van slid open, and a bunch of kids fell out and ran over to the table.

"Hey, Tommy, are you gonna trade your helicopter?"

"Yeah, and my 'rector set too."

"Yeah? I'm tradin' my gas station. Look, there's Snoopy!"

"Where? "

"In that carton, see? And a Mickey Mouse hat and a neat baseball mitt too."

"I wanna trade this 'rector set," Tommy said to Morgan. "And this 'copter too. How much will I get?"

"Let's see. The helicopter is in good condition. It's worth two fifty, easily. A dollar for the erector set. It's kind of beat-up. Two fifty and a dollar makes three fifty altogether."

"Can I get the Snoopy, the baseball mitt, *and* the Mickey hat for three fifty?"

Morgan thought about it. The glove was valued at a dollar fifty; the hat, a dollar. Snoopy was the extra-large size, and he was in great shape. They had valued him at two dollars even, so that came to four fifty. Morgan didn't hesitate. He knew how to operate. Like his dad always said, you had to think big, bigger than a few measly pennies. What were a few pennies compared to one satisfied customer? Satisfied customers came back and spent more money. You wound up making more than a few pennies that way.

"Give me an extra quarter, and you can have all three," he said to Tommy. "With the eighty-eight cents commission, that comes to a dollar thirteen."

The kid fished a bunch of loose change out of his pocket and started to count out nickels and dimes one at a time, laying them down on the table. P.J. shot Morgan a smile and said, "Right on, partner!" She was waiting on Tommy's sidekick, the one with the thousand-dollar miniature garage, complete with miniature gas pumps, hydraulic lift, mechanic's tools; even a stack of miniature spare tires and another of miniature oil cans.

Fergy, Mikey, and Sanford were all waiting on customers too. After hanging around with no customers for so long, they were knocking themselves out trying to please them.

More customers came, then more after them. In fact, customers kept on coming the whole afternoon. At one point Morgan glanced up, and there were four kids lined up behind the one he was waiting on. What was going on? First no customers, then, all at once, more than they could handle. It just went to prove his dad was right. You put in a lot of work in advance. Once you opened for business, there was nothing you could do but keep your fingers crossed. The rest was just a matter of luck.

The customers kept on coming. By three o'clock there was $30.42 in the cash box. Somehow you didn't think of all those pennies, nickels, dimes, and quarters that the customers kept handing you as a lot of money, but they all added up.

Morgan was waiting on a customer when he got one of his better brainstorms. The customer was in the market for old movie posters. Morgan said they didn't have any in stock. The customer asked if they might be getting some in. Morgan was about to reply that he didn't have the foggiest. Then his trusty light bulb went on, and he said, "Why don't you leave your name and phone number, and when we get some, we'll call you."

What a great idea! Offering their customers this extra personal service would keep them coming back again and again.

A little while later Morgan glanced over and saw Mikey signaling frantically to him. He went over to see what was up.

"See that kid over there?" Mikey whispered out of the side of his mouth, giving the big boy in the baseball jacket a furtive look. "He just snitched two tape cassettes."

Morgan sneaked a look at the boy. Man, he looked mean! "Did you actually see him take them?" he asked Mikey.

Mikey shook his head. "No, but I'm sure he did. Look at him. He even looks like a crook, shifty-eyed and sneaky."

"Mikey, what if you're wrong, and he didn't take them? You can't go around accusing people of stealing just because you don't like the way they look. For gosh sakes, you have to have something more substantial, witnesses who'll swear that they saw him do it, or evidence you found on his person when you searched him."

Mikey was all for walking over, collaring the boy, and searching him right then and there. Morgan managed to talk him out of it. "What do you want to be, a dead hero or a live millionaire?" he whispered in his ear. "Look at that kid, Mikey. He's three times your length and twice your width, easily. You'd have to have a black belt in karate to take on someone as big as that."

Morgan dragged Mikey away for a cold drink. Meanwhile the kid hung around, looking suspicious. Finally he left. They were both relieved.

"I was afraid you'd pick a fight with him," Morgan said to Mikey. "You would've been annihilated, and there would have been only three Turtles instead of four."

A little while later Mikey came over looking embarrassed. He shot Morgan a sheepish smile and held out his hand. In it were the two missing tapes. Mikey had found them in a carton under the table, where they had obviously fallen while he wasn't looking.

"See? Aren't you glad you didn't accuse the kid?" Morgan said. "You would have been accusing an innocent person, and you would have wound up getting slaughtered for no reason."

Morgan's last customer of the day was a kid he knew, a big kid from the neighborhood—Dean McLean. Dean said he was looking for a birthday present for his girl friend, but he wasn't looking awfully hard. He was asking Morgan questions, snooping for information. Morgan was no dope. He knew the score. He knew just what Dean was up to. When Dean said, "This is a good idea. I think I'll get a bunch of my friends together, and we'll open up a trading company for kids too," Morgan didn't overreact. He played it cool and acted as though he didn't even feel threatened by someone's going into competition with them. He put on a great big smile and said, "Lots of luck, but I hope you like hard work, long hours, and no money, because that's all you'll get in this business!"

When they were closing for the day, he said to the others, "Do you believe that Dean McLean? He was going to steal our idea and go into competition with us."

"Over my dead body!" P.J. declared angrily.

Fergy wasn't even mildly concerned. He said with a knowing smile, "Let him if he wants to, but he'll never make a success of it. Know why? Because he's not a Turtle!"

15

Chicken Soup
and
Celebration

"See? Didn't I tell you the business would be a success?" Morgan's dad said when he was driving them home. "Aren't you kids glad you listened to me and waited?"

"We sure are, Mr. Pierpont!" Mikey said, and grinned at Morgan from behind his hair. "As usual, you were right all along."

"We ought to go out and celebrate. What do you kids say to pizza at Rosati's?" Morgan's dad asked. The way he said it, he was obviously expecting them to flip over the idea. No one was flipping. They were all too tired to flip. Morgan's feet were killing him. He felt as though he had just jogged all the way to Big Bear Lake and back again nonstop.

"We're all too tired. How about some soup and sandwiches at our house, Dad?" he said, yawning loudly to accentuate his point.

"Snooky and the little guys want pizza, don't you, guys?" Sanford said to the tomato soup carton on his lap. He gave Morgan a dirty look to show what he thought of soup and sandwiches at home as opposed to pizza at Rosati's. They took a vote, and it was four against one.

"Tough luck, Sanford," Morgan sneered. "You got outvoted. By the way, since you don't happen to be a full-fledged Turtle just yet, you're not entitled to vote."

That shut Sanford up quick. All the rest of the way home he sulked and sucked his thumb. Morgan felt a little guilty. After the way Sanford had pitched right in and done his share all day, that had been a rather insensitive thing to say. He wanted to make it up to Sanford, so he said in a kinder tone, "Don't worry, we'll have pizza some other time when we're not so tired. I promise!"

Morgan's mom was in the kitchen. When Morgan told her about their day, she got excited. "It looks as though the Turtle Street Trading Company is here to stay," she said, and hugged him.

They were sitting around the table slurping up chicken noodle soup when Morgan's dad stood up and made a toast. "Here's to the Turtle Street Trading Company!"

It was a little difficult to drink a toast with a bowl of chicken noodle soup, so Morgan went and got the milk and some glasses instead. Aside from the pear at lunchtime, he hadn't eaten anything all day. And he was starving. He wound up having two bowls of soup plus three sandwiches. He was contemplating a fourth when his mom came in with the chocolate cake.

"Fergy's favorite!" Sanford exclaimed, and gave Fergy a poke.

Fergy didn't respond. He sat slumped in his chair, staring at his plate. There was a half-eaten sandwich on it.

"You okay, Ferg?" Morgan asked.

"Yeah. Sure. Don't I look okay?"

"No, not really."

Morgan's mom was passing the cake around. Fergy said he didn't want any. Fergy passing up chocolate cake? Now Morgan knew something was wrong! Maybe Fergy was coming down with something—something contagious. He could just picture it now: all the Turtles sick in bed, and the business going down the tubes for lack of someone to run it.

Morgan's mom rapped on the table and said, "Quiet, everybody! I have an announcement to make. I'm going to do a story about the Turtle Street Trading Company for next Sunday's People Section of *The Herald*."

Morgan jumped up and dashed around the table to kiss her. "Mom, you're the greatest!"

"No, that's Muhammad Ali." She laughed and kissed him back.

"You kids ought to think about renting a store," his dad remarked. "You can't go on doing business out of a parking lot indefinitely. It's too hard on your parents, the official company chauffeurs. Besides, what if we have a bad rainy season? That could put you right out of business. It just so happens there's a store that's about to become available right near Ralph's, the one on the end. I checked into it. It's a small store, mind you, but small store, small rent!"

"How do we know we'll make enough money to pay the rent every month?" P.J. asked worriedly.

"You don't," he replied. "At least not now. That's why I think you should wait awhile to make the decision, just until you have a better idea of where this business of yours is heading and what you can and can't afford."

"If we can't afford the store, maybe we could set up business in my garage," Mikey suggested.

"I don't think your parents would like that very much," Morgan's mom said.

"Yes, they would," Mikey replied with a grin.

"They're so glad I'm in the business, they'd even let us set up in the living room if we wanted to. See, this is the first time my dad ever saw me do anything but sit around and daydream. He says he was beginning to think daydreaming was going to be my full-time career when I grew up."

"After school starts, we'll only be open for business two days a week, on the weekends," P.J. reminded them.

"That will cut way down on our income. Even if we wind up making fifty dollars a day, we'll still be earning only a hundred a week."

"That's figuring on the low side, P.J., and on only being open two days a week," Morgan remarked. "Don't forget that Wednesday is a half day on account of parent-teacher conferences. School closes at noon. We could open at one and stay open until eight or so. That would give us one whole other day a week we'd be open for business and making money."

P.J. grinned and said to the others, "Morgan hasn't lost his touch. He's still got a few good ideas in him."

"A few? I've got a million of them," Morgan said, laughing, and helped himself to more cake. "Did I say a million? I meant a billion. Stick with me, you guys. Together we're going to be tycoons!"

16

Fergy's Dilemma

"Any new business?" Morgan asked after he had called the meeting to order the next morning.

Fergy started to say something, but Sanford, The Star, drowned him out with his singing:

> "Yippee ti yi yo,
> Git along, little dogies.
> It's your misfortune
> And none of my own.
> Yippee ti yi yo,
> Git along, little dogies.
> You know that Wyoming will be
> Your new home."

"I think it's Montana, not Wyoming," P.J. said

thoughtfully. "Or is it Colorado? I'm not sure."

"Colorado doesn't fit," Fergy told her. "It's got too many syllables." He started singing the song, substituting Colorado for Wyoming to prove his point.

"I'd like to go to Colorado," P.J. said, a dreamy look in her eyes.

"First let's go to Disneyland!" Sanford hollered at her.

On the question of when to go, everybody had a different opinion. P.J. said they should wait until after school started. Mikey agreed but thought they should go on a school holiday—Columbus Day, Martin Luther King's birthday, or Yom Kippur. Fergy said that Yom Kippur was a Jewish holiday, and the only place he would go on a Jewish holiday was to temple.

"And anyway," he concluded, "if you guys want me to go to Disneyland with you, you'd better plan on going before September first."

Nobody paid any attention. They just kept on debating the subject. Mikey took a bag of Sesame Crunch out of his pocket and started handing out candies.

"As I was saying," Fergy went on, stuffing two in his mouth at one time, "it better be before September first, or I won't be able to go."

He paused and waited for someone to react. When no one did, he continued. "I knew about it yesterday, but I didn't tell you. I didn't want to ruin your day. I mean, it was bad enough mine was ruined. Why should yours be too?" Mikey tossed him another candy. Fergy said,

"Thanks, pal! As I was saying, I thought it was nice of them to let me in on it. After all, it's only my life. Why should they bother to consult me? I'm just a kid, and nobody ever bothers to consult a kid on any subject, especially when it comes to deciding his own future."

"What's he talking about?" Mikey asked Morgan.

"You're asking me?" Morgan pointed to his forehead to show what he thought of Fergy's present mental state.

P.J. pretended to fall asleep from sheer boredom, but Fergy kept talking, complaining about how someone or other had mistreated him, but none of them had any idea how or why he had been mistreated, to say nothing of by whom.

"Nobody ever asks you. They just go right ahead and plan your whole future for you. After it's all been decided, they do you a favor and let you know what it's going to be. I bet you guys wouldn't like it either."

"Like what, Fergy?" Mikey asked, and tossed him another candy.

"Going to San Francisco to live," Fergy replied, tossing it back.

P.J. stopped snoring. She looked at Fergy and said,

"Who's going to San Francisco to live?"

"I am. That's what I just said, isn't it?"

"No. Not really. You said plenty of things, but that wasn't one of them."

"Yeah, well, that's what I meant. September first I'm going to San Francisco to live with my mom. See, it's like this. She's decided I can't stay here and live with my dad anymore, because he's too irresponsible. She says she can do a better job. My dad thinks so too. They got together and decided without even consulting me."

"This isn't really happening," Morgan muttered.

"Take my word for it, it is," Fergy assured him.

"But you can't go, Fergy. You can't move away from Turtle Street. That's in our club bylaws. 'No Turtle shall ever move away from Turtle Street and forsake his or her fellow Turtles'—Bylaw Number Three. There must be something we can do. We can't just sit by and let it happen."

Fergy just laughed. He was trying to act cool, as though the whole thing wasn't bothering him all that much, but Morgan knew him well enough to see through his act. Fergy was clever, but not clever enough to fool him. They had been friends too long for that.

P.J. offered a solution. "Maybe your dad will get so upset at the thought of your leaving, he'll start being responsible instead of irresponsible; maybe he'll go right out and get himself a steady job. That'll fix everything."

"Very funny!" Fergy sneered. "If he hasn't gotten around to doing it by now, it's pretty safe to say he isn't going to at this late date."

"Hold on a sec," P.J. went on, unwilling to give up. "What if our business is real, real successful, we make lots of money, and share some of it with your dad?"

"Yeah, I can just see him taking money from a bunch

of kids," Fergy said derisively. "Besides, that's only part of it. There are all those other things, too, like his never being around to make sure I do things—get to school on time and all."

"I've got it!" Sanford declared, practically jumping into Fergy's lap in his excitement. "You could come and live with us. Couldn't he, Morgan? Our parents wouldn't mind a bit. In fact they'd love it. They're always saying how they wish they had more kids."

Fergy smiled at Sanford. It was probably the world's saddest smile. It broke Morgan's heart to see Fergy this way. When he was low enough to open up and let you see how he felt, you knew he had hit rock bottom.

"I can't believe your father's going along with it," Morgan said.

"Neither can I," Fergy replied glumly. "But you know how he is—easygoing about things. I guess she talked him into it. I can't figure out why she changed her mind all of a sudden. When they got divorced, they had a friendly talk and decided we ought to live with Dad, since he was the one who had plenty of time to be with us. Mom was going up there to San Francisco to do her thing, start a whole new life, go to law school, and become a lawyer—something she dreamed about her whole life. It worked out great, us living with him and spending lots of weekends and vacations up there with her. But now all of a sudden she's all upset, saying Dad is irresponsible and a crummy parent, that he isn't looking after us or giving us the things he should. That's pure baloney! Being a good parent doesn't mean giving your kids lots of things. It means loving them a lot, and my Dad does. He's the greatest father in the world!"

Morgan didn't say anything. Fergy was pretty upset, and that would have upset him even more. But in Morgan's opinion, calling Mr. Weintraub the greatest father in the world was a gross exaggeration. He was a great guy, lots of fun to be with, more like a kid than an adult, but as for being a good father, he left a lot to be desired. A father should be dependable, mature, and responsible. He should be there for his kids when they needed him and make sure his kids had the things they needed and did things they were supposed to do. Mr. Weintraub was always taking off for parts unknown, leaving the kids alone. They were allowed to do as they pleased, and, especially in Fergy's case, that wasn't so terrific. Kids didn't always know what was best for them. That's why they needed parents. At least that was what Morgan thought.

The thought of life without Fergy was awful, but Morgan had to admit he could see why Fergy's mother wanted him to live with her. The only trouble was that, even though it might be the best thing for Fergy, it was going to be the worst thing for the Turtles.

17

Turtles
Make News!

"LOCAL KIDS TURN OLD JUNK INTO BIG BUSINESS," the headline in Sunday's edition of *The Herald* said. There was his mom's byline underneath—"by Sarah Weatherby Pierpont"—and a photograph of the Turtles in all their glory standing behind their table, Ralph's parking lot in the background. Under the picture was a caption, *The Turtle Street Tycoons*, and their names, only it said Priscilla Jane Alberoy instead of P.J. Morgan knew old P.J. was going to be thrilled to pieces about that.

CALABASAS, Ca., July 29—What has five parts, a total age of fifty-six, is noisy, boisterous, sloppy, awfully smart, and makes a lot of money?

Give up? The answer is the Turtle Street Trading Company.

The Turtle Street Trading Company is the brainstorm of Morgan J. Pierpont III, president of a social club from Calabasas known as the Turtles. The Turtles, four twelve-year olds and an eight-year-old, started out as friends. Now they are business partners, co-owners of a unique business that's the talk of the West Valley, one that's revolutionizing the toy industry by turning used toys and other things kids buy (or get their parents to buy for them) into a very desirable commodity.

The Turtles can be found providing their unique service to their customers in the parking lot of the Mulview Shopping Center at Mulwood and San Luis roads every day from Tuesday through Sunday, ten A.M. until six P.M.

Kids come by the carload from all over to trade their used toys, tapes, records, posters, models, T-shirts, and other articles for similar things brought in by other kids. The Turtles turn it all into dollars for themselves.

In the week since their grand opening on Saturday, July 21, they have made over $300. That's over and above their initial overhead costs, which, the Turtles are the first to admit, are pretty low, since they pay no rent, hire no employees, need no equipment to run their business, and depend on their parents for free food and transportation.

After repaying two business loans, the Turtles plan to spend some of their profits on a trip to Disneyland. After that, the future looks bright for these ambitious, hardworking youngsters from Calabasas. As President Morgan J. Pierpont III told this reporter during an interview at his home on Turtle Street recently, "Who knows? The Turtles may decide to go public, maybe even start a franchise operation nationwide—a whole bunch of Turtle Street Trading Companies all around the country."

In the meantime the Turtles are enjoying their unexpected, and unprecedented, success. As President Pierpont's younger brother Sanford Ronald Pierpont so aptly put it, "There's nothing us Turtles can't do so long as we all stick together!"

That last line really tugged at the old heartstrings! His mom had written the article prior to Fergy's announcing his premature departure from their midst. Already Turtle Togetherness was a thing of the past.

Morgan's dad took him to the discount drugstore and had a hundred copies of the article run off on the copying machine. Morgan was going to hand them out as advertisements. He was also going to make a scrapbook and put a copy of the article in it, along with other souvenirs, mementos, and remembrances of the business. The way things were going, that could easily turn out to be the only thing they would have to remember Turtle Street Trading Company by.

Sanford thought he was a celebrity now that his picture had been in the paper. He cut it out and tacked it up on the bulletin board in their room. Over it he tacked a piece of construction paper on which he had printed in his big baby scrawl, *FAMOUSE TURTEL SANFORD R. PIERPONT & FREINDS.*

Morgan's dad kept bragging about his sons, the big businesspersons. He said he was going to have copies of the article framed so he could hang them in prominent spots in his stores where everybody who came in could see them.

Now that the business was a success, he said, there were some things the Turtles needed to know about running it properly. How to keep records, for instance. They would need to refer to those records when it came time for them to pay their yearly income taxes.

Income taxes? Morgan hadn't thought about those. He knew his dad paid them, but he hadn't realized the Turtles would have to. He was pretty annoyed at the whole idea of sharing his hard-earned money with the government. If the government wasn't going to do any of the work, how come it got a share of the profits?

His dad explained that the government collected taxes from every American citizen in order to get the money to run the country with and provide all the services it made available, services without which there wouldn't be a country to run. When you thought about it, it made sense to give the government its fair share. If not for the government, and the freedom it provided, people wouldn't be entitled to go into business for themselves in the first place.

"How much money will we have to give the government?" Morgan asked his dad. He hoped not too much. He had big plans for that money.

"It all depends on how much you make," his dad replied. "It could be fifteen or twenty percent. If you make a whole lot of money from your business, it could even be fifty. Don't worry," he added when he saw Morgan flinch. "When the time comes for you to fill out your income-tax returns, we'll hire a good accountant to help you. That's what accountants do: help other people deal with the complicated business of handling their money. And accountants are thoroughly acquainted with how the Internal Revenue Service and the tax system work."

The Turtles had a few crazy days after the newspaper article came out. Everybody and his brother called to congratulate them on their sudden notoriety. And they all asked the same dumb questions:

How does it feel to be a tycoon?

What are you going to do with all that money?

Why don't you lend some of it to me?

When are your parents going to retire and let you kids support them?

At least Morgan's uncle Herbie came up with something a little more original:

How about buying your old uncle a shiny new Mercedes

45O-SL *now that you're so rich? Red, please with a white convertible top.*

A lot of people must have read that article, because customers came in droves the next day. There were so many of them that the Turtles were inundated, and their parents had to organize a work force and come down to the parking lot in shifts to help out. Even Mr. Weintraub took a turn. He was a much better Turtle than he was a used-car salesman.

That night the Turtles went out to celebrate. They had a big Mexican dinner at the Purple Onion, then went to see a double-feature at the Calabasas Cinema—*Look Out Behind You!* plus *Killer Cargo*, a movie about a load of cargo that comes up from the hold, oozes over everything in sight, and massacres the captain, his crew, and every last one of the passengers on a cruise ship.

Except for Sanford, everyone enjoyed the movies a lot. Sanford didn't even see them. He spent the whole three hours under his seat. He kept poking Morgan and whispering, "What's happening now?" But he wouldn't come out to see for himself. He was too scared. Morgan was just as glad. If there was one thing he didn't need, it was Sanford having nightmares and keeping him up all night.

18

An Offer
No Turtle Can
Refuse

Morgan's mom had to go to a press conference at the mayor's office in the city, so she couldn't drive them to the parking lot on Tuesday morning. His dad couldn't either. He had to be at the store early to start his inventory. Mr. Weintraub offered to take them, but he couldn't stick around and help them get set up. He had a job interview to go to. Morgan couldn't help wondering what kind of job interview he could be going to dressed in ragged jeans and a Yogi Bear T-shirt.

"He's not going to any old interview," Fergy said bitterly when his dad drove off in the pickup truck. "He's going to the beach again, but he's too ashamed to admit it."

"Maybe the job he's interviewing for is the job of life guard," Mikey suggested in his usual helpful way.

Fergy just looked at him and said, "Nuts to that!" While the others were setting up, he went to Alice's Bakery, bought a box of fudge brownies, sat down on the curb, and proceeded to eat every last one himself.

It turned out to be another busy day in the brief but successful history of the Turtle Street Trading Company. They were so busy, they couldn't even take time off to eat lunch. They had to take turns running to the deli for take-out stuff. Then they couldn't sit down to eat. They had to grab bites between customers.

Morgan didn't eat his lunch until two thirty. He was just polishing off a big pastrami on rye from Goldie's Deli when a nifty red sports car pulled up, and a little woman climbed out and walked over to the table. She had on an enormous straw hat, floppy flowered pants that tied around her ankles, and the highest pair of high heels he had ever seen. Even with them on she was tiny, not more than five feet tall at most. When she took off her hat, he got a good look at her face. It looked familiar, but he couldn't remember where he had seen it before.

"Whew! This is what I call hot!" she gasped, and started fanning herself with the hat. "Is it always this hot out here in the valley?"

"It's always at least ten degrees warmer than in the city," Fergy informed her.

She smiled at him, stuck out her hand, and said, "You're Morgan J. Pierpont the third, right?"

"Wrong! I'm Ferguson Weintraub the first. That's Morgan J. Pierpont over there," Fergy replied, and pointed at Morgan.

She looked at Morgan and shook her head. "Uh, uh! You're definitely not a Morgan. You like about as much like a Morgan as I do!"

"My parents did consider calling me Preston," Morgan said, and smiled lamely at her.

"No. Preston is out. I think Rock or Lance or Brett would be more appropriate."

"Brett's okay, I guess. I don't mind Lance, but Rock is definitely out. It's just not me."

She hoisted up one pants leg and sat down on the edge of the table. She had a smile right out of a toothpaste ad on TV. Suddenly he knew where he had seen that face before.

"You're Millie Millhouse from Channel 2!"

"You got it! And I drove all the way out here in this heat wave to ask you and the other Turtles if you'd like to be on my show."

"The Turtles on TV? " Morgan exclaimed.

Sanford pushed his way past him. "Hi, Millie! How ya' doin'? I'm Sanford R. Pierpont. The *R* stands for Ronald. You know what? You're a lot prettier in person than on TV."

"Who's he, your press agent?" Ms. Millhouse laughed.

Morgan shook his head. "My kid brother. Ignore

him, and maybe he'll go away."

Instead of going away, Sanford did his Gary Coleman imitation for Ms. Millhouse. She thought he was terrific. "You'll be *dyn-no-mite* on my show," she said to him.

"Dynamite, huh? Let's light his fuse and blow him up," Morgan muttered.

"I could do my Gary Coleman imitation on your show," Sanford said to Ms. Millhouse, and socked it to her with his pearly whites.

She shook her head. "There won't be enough time, Sanford Ronald, but just do yourself, okay? The audience will love you just the way you are. You'll be a star!"

Without even waiting for them to say yes or no, she started making all kinds of plans. "Let's see....When should we tape the interview?" she said to herself. Then she answered her own question. "Friday!"

"So soon?" P.J. croaked. You could tell by her face that she was on the verge of hysteria. Frantic wasn't even the word.

Ms. Millhouse didn't seem to notice. "My crew and I will be here Friday morning, bright and early," she said. "Don't do anything you don't usually do. Don't get all dressed up or anything. Be natural, and you'll be a hit."

It didn't occur to her that they might not want to do it. She just took it for granted that they did and acted accordingly. They were all so overwhelmed that they didn't enlighten her.

"Do you want to do it?" Morgan said to the others after she had driven away.

"I don't!" P.J. declared.

"Neither do I," Mikey added, and he looked scared as anything.

"How can we turn down an opportunity like this?" Fergy said. "Think of all that free publicity."

"He's right," Morgan agreed. "We have to do it. We'd be crazy not to."

"Besides, I want to be a star! " Sanford informed them. "You gotta do it for *me*."

Sanford was convinced he was already a star. He went around driving everybody nuts with his imitations. In addition to Gary Coleman, John Wayne, Darth Vader, and Mickey Mouse, he had added Donald Duck to his repertoire, so now there were five.

"My boys on TV!" Morgan's mom cried when they told her. "My babies on TV!"

"Think of all that free publicity," Morgan's dad said. You could hear cash registers ringing softly in the background.

Morgan and his parents were in the den playing Scrabble. For obvious reasons Morgan was having a little difficulty keeping his mind on the game. It was his dad's turn, and, as usual, he was taking his time about it. After five whole minutes of deliberation, he picked up a tile and put it down on the board at the end of the word

Morgan had just made, turning *bull* into *bully*.

"As in *bully for you!*" he was kind enough to explain.

"Or *big bully*, a tough guy who pushes little guys around."

"Very good, dear," Morgan's mom said. She studied the board for half a minute before making her move, to put *awn* on the board going downward from the *y* in *bully*, making *yawn*.

Morgan already knew what he was going to do. He used the *b* in bully, added *ear*, and made *bear*.

Sanford came in and started sounding out the words on the board. "B-e-a-r is for *bear*! Why don't you put a teddy up above it and make it *teddy bear*, Morgan?"

"Why don't you mind your own beeswax, Sanford?" Morgan mimicked. "You're not in this game." When they were upstairs getting ready for bed, he said, "I'm going to set the alarm for seven, okay?"

"So early? Why do you want to get up so early, Morgan?"

"I don't want to have to rush around and get more nervous than I already am."

"Nervous? About *what*, Morgan?"

"Oh, nothing! Just because we're going on TV, why should I be nervous? After all, it's no big deal. We do it every other day. By the way, Sanford The Star, I forgot to tell you. Johnny Carson called you up while you were in the bathtub to ask you if you would be on his show."

19

Lights, Action, Camera!

Morgan got up early, showered, shampooed his hair, and got all dressed up in his best cut offs, his new jogging shoes, his striped knee-high Rugby socks, his Turtles T-shirt, and his Dodgers baseball cap, which he wore turned around backward because it looked so cool.

Sanford insisted on wearing his Mickey Mouse costume, ears and all.

The show aired at eight P.M. on Friday. Ms. Millhouse had told them to meet her and her crew at nine A.M. sharp in the parking lot to tape their segment. They had to get it done and over with early, she said, because the crew had another one to tape out in Agoura, and they had to be there before eleven.

The Turtles were all set up and ready at eight thirty.

P.J. looked like a walking strawberry patch in a frilly white dress with little strawberries embroidered all over it. You could see how miserable and uncomfortable she was by the way she kept yanking and pulling at it.

Mikey had broken down and gotten a haircut especially for the occasion. For the first time in months you could actually see his face.

Fergy looked like a big game hunter from Africa in khaki shorts and a matching bush jacket. All he needed was a pith helmet.

Ms. Millhouse and her crew didn't show up until almost ten. By that time the Turtles were so nervous they could hardly function. The customers didn't seem to notice. They kept giving them their money anyway.

Ms. Millhouse arrived in her nifty sports car. Her crew came in a psychedelic hearse. To say they were a little different would be a gross understatement. They were a lot different, about as different as Morgan had ever encountered in his life.

To start off with, they all spoke to one another in a strange language. Oh, it was English—just not any kind of English Morgan had ever heard before, that's all. They kept saying things like "Far *in*, man!" "Go with the flow," "Cosmic flood," and "Tube it or tape it, baby." They wore very odd clothes. One guy had on a striped prison uniform. Another was all dressed up like a police officer. There was a girl in short shorts and shocking pink roller skates. She skated around doing all sorts of things with a light meter. Every time she skated past Morgan, she looked at him as if she expected him to light up and become incandescent. When he asked her what she was doing, she said, "Electrifying, baby!" and skated away.

"Don't mind my crew," Ms. Millhouse whispered to him. "They're a little weird, but they do good work."

He couldn't see that any of them was working. They sat around on the asphalt smoking cigarettes and drinking coffee. After a few minutes Ms. Millhouse stuck two fingers in her mouth and gave out a shrill whistle, and everybody jumped up and started racing around. Morgan glanced at Ms. Millhouse. She may have been little, but she sure packed a lot of punch!

A girl carrying a portable TV camera climbed out of the hearse. She was wearing a silver jumpsuit, silver boots, and silver cap with a visor and wings on it. "All set, Millie. Let's go for it!" she said.

The guy in the prison uniform handed Millie a microphone with a cord about a thousand yards long. The cord was hooked up inside the hearse.

Morgan felt his mouth go dry. His legs were wobbly.

Millie dazzled the camera with her billion-dollar smile and said, "This is Millie Millhouse. Welcome to *Talk of the Town!*"

Morgan's stomach rolled over and played dead. Ms.

Millhouse kept talking to that camera as though it were her best friend, as if she were in her living room, not on TV.

"Today you'll meet a man who runs a horse ranch in Agoura. We'll take you on a tour of a Chinese egg-roll factory in Compton, and introduce you to four—make that *five*—genuine kid tycoons from Calabasas."

Morgan sneaked a quick peek at Fergy. His face was a little green. Mikey's was red as a beet. P.J.'s just looked flash frozen. The only one who looked normal was good old soon-to-be-famous-TV-star Sanford Ronald Pierpont!

"Meet the Turtles," Ms. Millhouse said, "co-owners of a business that's making headlines. It's called the Turtle Street Trading Company, and it's founded on a rather unique concept, the recycling of kids' toys and all that other junk your kids and mine are constantly getting us to spend our hard-earned money on."

The camera was creeping in closer and closer. Morgan had an almost irresistible urge to turn and run for the hills.

"In case you didn't read all about them in Sunday's *Herald*, here are the Turtles." Ms. Millhouse proceeded to introduce them to the TV audience. Morgan had a terrible feeling she was going to talk to him first. He had written and rehearsed a speech, but he couldn't remember a word of it now. Suddenly that microphone was in front of his nose, and she was saying, "President

Morgan J. Pierpont the third is only twelve, but he has a forty-year-old head, a head for big business. Tell me, Morgan, how does it feel to be a teen-aged tycoon?"

"It's pretty exciting, Ms. Hillhouse," he heard himself say in a voice like a chipmunk's. "But it's a lot of hard work too!"

There were a few giggles from the customers, who were standing off to one side watching the taping. Morgan wished he knew the magic word so he could say it and disappear in a puff of smoke. She was asking him about the business. He started to explain. Parts of the speech were coming back to him. If he could only remember not to stop breathing, he was home free!

She was asking him another question. "Was being rich and famous what the Turtles had in mind when they first started the business?"

"Oh, no!" he was saying in that high-pitched chipmunk's voice. "All we wanted was to make enough money so we could go to Disneyland, and the funny thing about that is, now that we have, we can't go. We're too busy."

"I don't want to pry," she said to Fergy, the great lion hunter, "but just how much money have you kids made since you started the business?"

Fergy's voice came out more like a croak. Now he didn't just look like a frog. He sounded like one too. "As of yesterday, a little over seven hundred dollars, Ms. Millhouse," he said, and blinked at the camera from behind his spectacles. Any minute you expected him to say *"Rivet!"* and leap-frog away.

"That's a lot of money in two weeks. Tell me, what are you going to do with your share of the profits?"

"Spend it, I guess."

"On what?"

"Oh, *things*, like a new bike. Maybe a hang glider and a surfboard. Some new furniture for my dad. A new pickup for my dad. His is a rolling junk heap...."

He would have gone on indefinitely, but she moved the microphone to P.J. and asked, "What about *you*, P.J.?"

"I'm go—going to b-b-buy a h-horse ranch in Ariz—zona!" P.J. stammered.

Ms. Millhouse asked Mikey, and he launched into a long monologue about the joys of nature exploring.

When it came his turn, Morgan had his answer all ready. "I'm going to use it to reinvest in other businesses. I have a lot of very innovative ideas I'd like to see developed, all under the Turtles' logo and all designed with today's youth in mind. By the time I'm grown up, I plan to have a business empire nationwide, and it will have all started right here in this parking lot with the Turtle Street Trading Company!"

20

Turtles on TV

The girl in the silver jumpsuit lowered her camera. "Okay, everybody, that's a wrap!"

The customers, who had been standing off to one side, guarded by the guy in the prison stripes and the phony policeman, broke loose, converged on Ms. Millhouse, and started asking her for her autograph. The crew started to pack up and get ready to leave.

"You were wonderful, Turtles!" Ms. Millhouse said. "Morgan, I meant to ask you one more question, but there wasn't time. Will you marry me?"

In all the excitement, they had forgotten about The Star, but he made his presence felt—and heard—by having a tantrum right in front of everybody.

"I did-dent get to talk on TV!" he wailed between heartrending sobs.

"Oh, Sanford, how could I have overlooked you?" Ms. Millhouse said, horrified at the oversight. "Hold on a sec, Charlene," she called to the Silver Streak. "I want to add another minute. We can work it in when we get back to the studio."

"It's your ball game, Millie," the Silver Streak said, and came trotting back, camera in hand.

Morgan was trying to get Sanford calmed down, but he wasn't having much luck. Sanford wasn't just pretending. He was really upset. Morgan set his Mickey Mouse ears on straight and smiled reassuringly at him.

Ms. Millhouse stuck the microphone under Sanford's bright red nose and said, "Smile, Sanford!"

Sanford stopped blubbering. In fact he stopped doing everything. He stood there staring at that camera as if he were hypnotized. He looked a lot like a statue Morgan had once seen in the Los Angeles Museum.

Millie turned on that super-duper smile of hers. "Ladies and gentlemen, meet Sanford Pierpont. Sanford is eight and, not unlike his older brother Morgan, he's definitely not your average, garden-variety kid by any stretch of the imagination. But wait. I'll let him demonstrate that for himself. Speak, Sanford!" she commanded, as though she were talking to a performing poodle and not a person. "Tell our viewers what you want to be when you grow up—which is going to be day after tomorrow, I think, ladies and gentlemen," Millie added as an aside for her fans.

She was probably expecting Sanford to say something humorous, like he wanted to grow up to be a star— John Wayne or Mickey Mouse. If that's what she was expecting, she must have been disappointed. Sanford didn't say anything humorous. He didn't say anything at all. He just stood there staring at that camera, transfixed with terror. Morgan was pretty sure he was still alive. Wasn't that him breathing into the microphone like Darth Vader? Aside from the breathing, there were no discernible signs of life from Sanford Ronald Pierpont, almost-star.

Ms. Millhouse gave it another try, but it was no use. Either Sanford had lost his voice or had left his body altogether.

"Sanford blew it," Morgan said to his parents when they came to pick him up. "He blew his big chance at stardom, but Ms. Millhouse said the next time we go on her show, he can do his Gary Coleman routine. Some producer will catch his act and sign him up."

Morgan's mom phoned everyone in the civilized world to tell them the Turtles were going to be on TV. The entire neighborhood was coming to Morgan's house to watch the show. His dad was taping it on a video recorder borrowed from Mr. Nagura, the man who owned the TV and appliance store down the street from the Pierponts' party supply store in Woodland Hills. Morgan couldn't wait to see himself on TV.

"I handled myself like a pro," he told his grandmother when she called up to congratulate him. "I was as relaxed as anything. It was easy. All I did was pretend the camera wasn't there."

When his dad was hooking up the equipment, Fergy leaned over to him and whispered, "*Nice*. Your dad's taping the show for posterity. That way, when you're all grown up, you'll be able to look back and see what a total jerk you made of yourself on TV when you were twelve. I especially enjoyed that part when you called Ms. Millhouse *Ms. Hillhouse*. That was particularly memorable!"

Fergy and his dad had come a little early so Mr. Weintraub could set up his equipment. He was taping the show for posterity, too, but only the sound portion. Mr. and Mrs. McGrath and P.J.'s mom and stepfather came together. Morgan helped his mom serve fruit and cheese and crackers. The only one who wanted any was Fergy. He started with a plate full of fruit and never stopped eating the rest of the evening.

At ten to eight Morgan's dad switched on the set. They had to sit through the last minutes of some dumb sitcom, then a bunch of boring commercials. Finally the theme music for *Talk of the Town* came on, followed by those great aerial shots of L.A. that they always showed at the start of the show. Then, after that, a close-up of Millie and her billion-dollar smile.

"This is Millie Millhouse. Welcome to *Talk of the Town!*"

P.J. grabbed a pillow, stuck it over her face, and cried, "I refuse to watch! It's too horrible."

When Millie started talking about that egg-roll factory in Compton, Mr. McGrath leaned over to Morgan's dad and whispered, "I hope the kids are on first. I'm not too keen on egg rolls."

Fergy and Morgan exchanged glances, then ducked their heads to keep from laughing. The camera was panning away from Millie and focusing on the Turtles. Morgan slid down behind the coffee table. P.J. was right. It was too horrible. Did he really look so scrawny? So short? So young? Some pro!

Oh, no! Now Millie was asking him how it felt to be a teen-aged tycoon, and he was answering, in a voice like a chipmunk's, "It's pretty exciting, Ms. Hillhouse."

Fergy nudged him with his elbow. "They ought to give you your own prime-time show, Pierpont. You're a class act!"

"Very amusing, big bwana!" Morgan couldn't wait until Fergy turned into a frog on television. "You're on, Froggy!" he croaked when the incredible jumping frog from Calabasas appeared on the screen.

P.J. stammered her one-liner. Mikey did his Joys of Nature monologue. Then Morgan came back on and did his Big Business Entrepreneur routine.

"Those are the Turtles," Millie said. "And now back to our studio for a commercial message."

"Weren't they cute?" Mrs. McGrath gushed as all the grown-ups repaired to the dining room for a coffee break.

P.J. emerged from behind her pillow and asked, "Is it all over? Can I come out now?"

"Come out, come out, wherever you are!" Mikey said, and went to turn off the set.

"Hold on a sec," Morgan said. "Millie might say something else."

Right on cue Millie came back on and said, "I have a postscript to that story about those kid tycoons from Calabasas. This afternoon I got a phone call from the president of the group, Morgan J. Pierpont, telling me about a problem the Turtles have been having, but why don't I let Morgan explain it to you himself?"

"Why don't you?" Morgan said with a smile.

The camera swung to the right and panned in for a close-up of him lounging in a chair by Millie's side.

"What's he doing there?" P.J. whispered to Mikey.

"I ought to explain about the Turtles first," the Morgan on TV was saying. "See, we're not just business partners. We're best friends. More than friends actually. We're Turtles!"

He went on to explain about the club, then about Fergy's dilemma. "It was a terrible shock to all of us to discover that we were about to lose a fellow Turtle," he said to Ms. Millhouse. "For a while there it looked like the end of the line for the Turtles, but then I stumbled on a way to save the Turtles from becoming extinct. It suddenly occurred to me that if we were to open up a branch of the business in San Francisco with Ferguson Weintraub at its helm, we wouldn't be losing a fellow Turtle. We'd be gaining a branch of the Turtle Street Trading Company!"

21

Turtles Together Forever!

The camera panned away, and Millie said, "That was Morgan J. Pierpont, president of the Turtle Street Trading Company and a good friend of mine. Now here's a message from another good friend, the German Meal Baking Company."

Morgan stuck his face in front of the screen and lisped, "Th-th-that's *all*, folks!" Then he hummed the theme music from the Porky Pig cartoon.

"When did you tape that part?" Mikey asked from under the rocker.

"A couple of hours ago. My mom drove me to the studio, and Millie promised to put it on right after our interview. Pretty neat, huh? The miracle of modern technology!"

"Gee, you sure are smart, Morg," Mikey said adoringly.

"Wish I was smart like you. Then I could come up with terrific ideas too."

"You're doing okay, Mikey," Morgan replied. Remember, it was you who came up with the name for our business."

"Yeah, that was a pretty good idea, if I do say so myself," Mikey exclaimed.

Fergy gave Morgan's latest brainstorm the thumbs-down signal right off the bat. When Morgan asked him why, he said, "Because it's crummy, that's why. But seriously, folks, you didn't mean it, did you, Pierpont? You were just joshing when you said that about us opening up a branch of the business up there?"

"Would I go on TV and joke about a thing like that?" Morgan replied.

"I don't know. Would you? I hope so, because, for your information, there isn't going to be any branch of the business in San Francisco."

"Why not?" P.J. asked.

"Because I can't do it, that's why not, birdbrain," Fergy said disgruntledly.

"Did you hear what I heard?" P.J. said incredulously.

"Naw, I must be hearing things!"

Fergy, the original Kid Confidence, having doubts about himself? It didn't seem possible. "You could do it with your eyes closed and both hands tied behind your back," Morgan said to him.

"Morgan's right. It'd be a cinch!" P.J. added.

"If it'd be such a cinch, why don't you do it, Miss Priscilla Jane?" Fergy simpered at her.

She didn't even get mad at him for calling her Priscilla Jane. She smiled blandly at him and replied, "Because I'm not the one who's moving to San Francisco, that's why. Weintraub, don't be dumb. You could do it. It'd be easy as pie, a lot easier than when we started out. You'd have money to start out with, plus experience. You wouldn't be a greenhorn like we were. All you'd have to do is scout out a good location, find a few kids to help you, and you'd be in business."

"Oh, is that all?" he said.

"We'd be here for you to consult with if you ran into any problems," Morgan added, "just a phone call away. By the way, that reminds me. I must ask my dad if we're allowed to take phone calls off our income taxes," he added in a more practical frame of mind.

Mikey came up with another brainstorm. That made two in a row. "You know how business people are always traveling around on business? They hop on a plane, and off they go. We could fly back and forth between Los Angeles and San Francisco all the time. We'd be airborne!"

"Flying Turtles!" Sanford said, and started to soar around the room like an airplane in flight, making aeronautical noises. "We'll buy our own plane. We'll call it the Turkletaub."

Morgan put an arm around Fergy's shoulders. "If you

only had as much faith in yourself as we have in you, you'd know you could do it."

"You really think so? " Fergy asked.

"I don't think so. I know so! Look what a contribution you've made to the Turtle Street Trading Company. What makes you think you can't do that again?"

"Maybe I could if you guys were with me," Fergy said, "but not on my own." You could tell he was all broken up. "I know you want me to do it," he added, "and I'd like to be able to do it for that reason. Maybe I could give it a try. I'm not promising anything, you understand," he said hastily when he saw they were about to celebrate his decision. "All I'm saying is I'll give it my best shot. If it doesn't work out, don't blame me, because I told you so!"

"Does that mean he's gonna do it?" Mikey asked P.J.

"I think so," P.J. replied.

"He's gonna do it, Morg," Mikey said.

"I know that. You know that. Sanford and P.J. know that, but does Fergy know that?" Morgan laughed.

"I'm gonna do it!" Fergy announced. His fist shot up in the air, making the secret signal. "Turtles together forever!"

Morgan, P.J., and Mikey raised their fists. "Turtles together forever!" they said in unison.

Sanford had to get in on the act. He raised his fist and made a reasonable facsimile of the secret signal, only his pinky stuck out a little, so it looked more like a snail's head than a turtle's. "Turtles forever together?" he exclaimed. It was a question, not a statement of fact.

Morgan shook his head. "Uh, uh, Sanford. No way. You can't say the secret motto. You're not a full-fledged Turtle."

"Not yet?" You could see Sanford was crushed. His face crumpled. His body seemed to sag. You knew any minute he'd be crying his head off.

Morgan put him out of his misery. He reached under the couch and pulled out the box he had hidden there earlier.

Sanford stared at it. "What's in it? he asked in a tremulous voice.

"Why don't you open it and find out?" Morgan said. Sanford opened the box. When he saw what was inside, he started dancing around in a frenzy, clutching it to his chest, yelling "Yippee yahooey!" Inside the box was a T-shirt, a purple one with a green turtle outlined in orange on the chest.

Morgan ran after Sanford and tried to grab his hand so he could shake it and formally welcome him into the club, but Sanford wouldn't stand still long enough. "Well, anyway, welcome to the club, Sanford. Today you are a Turtle," Morgan said with a shrug, and went back to the couch to sit down.

"Welcome to the club, Sandy. The Duke would be mighty proud of you today," P.J. said.

"You're finally a full-fledged Turtle, Sanford," Mikey said. "I'm glad!"

"You deserve it too," Fergy added. "You're a good worker, Sanford. You've made a big contribution to the business. We're all proud of you."

Sanford finally came down from Cloud Nine. "Gee, thanks, you guys. You'll never know how much this means to me," he said emotionally. Anyone could see how overwhelmed he was by the honor bestowed on him. Eager to prove he was really one of them at last, he came over, stuck his fist in Morgan's face and exclaimed, "*Turkletaub!*"

"It's *Turtletaub*, not *Turkletaub*, Sanford," Morgan said, laughing. "And when you make the secret signal, tuck your thumb under all four fingers, like this." He raised his fist and made the secret signal to show Sanford. "Turtles together forever!" he said.

The other Turtles raised their fists on high. One by one they touched fists with the new member. Solemnly they repeated the motto, "Turtles together forever!" It seemed to have taken on a whole new meaning for them now.

Morgan smiled to himself. "What a beautiful ceremony, and what a special moment in all our lives," he thought a little wistfully. He had a feeling they would all have reason to remember it in the future.

"Well, Sanford, you're finally one of us, a full-fledged Turtle," he said to his little brother. "I'm glad you made it. To tell the truth, I always wanted a Turtle for a brother."